THE DRAGLEN BROTHERS SERIES

BOOK 3

SOLEASE M BARNER

Copyright © 2014 by Solease M Barner

ISBN-13: 978-1500630430

ISBN-10: 1500630438

Editing: Tabitha Ormiston-Smith

THANK YOU

Thank you to all those who continue to support my books. I'm always happy to see people enjoying the worlds I create. Thanks for supporting me always.

Thank you to Barner's Beautiful Divas, you ladies are the best! I love chatting with each of you and I have to say you shock me with how much support you show for my books. I have the best street team and you all are awesome DIVAS!!!

THANK YOU TO SOME VERY SPECIAL PEOPLE:

Teresa Muncus you are fabulous! All the work you do for me behind the scenes is so appreciated. I think I would forget my head if you didn't remind me where it is lol. Thank you, and I look forward to working with you even more!!

Annmarie Young, you are the pimp queen when it comes to books!! Thank you for including me while you promote books, I'm very happy you choose my books to pimp. ☺

Cathy Lasky I love all you do for me and I enjoy knowing you are on my side. I love all the special things. Thank you!

Colleen Everly you truly ROCK! Thank you!

Kera Montgomery thanks for your help, you do so much without complaints, I appreciate you!

Renita McKinney, first, thank you for trusting me. That trust has blossomed into so much more than you being just a reader. Thanks for giving advice and supporting my books, I appreciate it!

THE TEAM THAT MAKES IT HAPPEN!

Tabitha, you are more than an editor to me, you are the teacher that I never had. I've learned so much having you work on my books. Thank you so much for teaching me and I love that you learn new things from me during editing. During editing I think you hate me, but I know you only want the best for me. I look forward to the next book with you.

Patti, I tell you all the time you are heaven sent and you always prove my point. It's always a joy to work on covers, swag and banners with you. I smile every time, knowing you will be patient and kind, and you always make sure that I'm happy with the cover even if it means changing it around lots of times. Thanks Patti, we have more work to do!

SPECIAL THANKS

I have to thank my heavenly father Jesus for giving me the talent to write. I would not be here if it wasn't for my faith in him. I would like to thank my husband for standing by me always, and dealing with the long hours I spend writing. I love you, sweetie! To my only child Princess Shaniya, it's such a joy to see you every day. You are my heart! Thank you to my family and friends who are always supportive with me writing I love you all. My SWH you are awesome and I love that you still drink wine with me as I read you all my ideas, it's always fun.

If I have missed someone, I would like to say now I thank everyone who is loving and supporting me and my books. I have a special place in my heart for all this love and support!

Now I hope you enjoy LAYERN - Book 3

REVIEWS FROM BETA READERS

BETA 1, 5 stars- I love my hot Dragons. Solease M Barner has once again gifted me with an awesome read. Brother number 3 Layern I could not put down my kindle (also had the same problem with Draken & Showken) Layern and Reseda's story tore at my heart strings I loved the fact he was willing to give up everything to have her. I would say this is my favorite book so far. I also loved the fact we got to catch up with Draken and Showken. I felt still involved in their lives.

BETA 2, I was lucky enough to get to be a Beta reader for this book. Finally we get Layern's story. He has been one of my favorites among the brothers, so I am so glad I got to read his story. It was fun seeing him get frustrated with Reseda because he couldn't read her at first. It was just as funny to see her get upset because Layern would answer her questions once they were intimate and he could get a good read on her. The dynamics between the family members just get better and better with each book. I love how the ladies interact with each other. Making Reseda the godmother to the Youngling was just the sweetest. All in all a great book.

BETA 3, 5 stars all the way around! Loved Layern's story. Definitely a hard book to put down. I was very intrigued by Layern, and just his story hooked me from the get go. Solease has done it yet once again. Glad to read it. Makes me love all the Draglen brothers even more. I loved that she kept Draken and Showken in his story here and there so it made you feel that you could stay connected to all of the brothers we have read about. Can't wait to see where the next chapter of the brothers leads us to.

BETA 4, 5 stars Layern and Reseda. This is book 3 in The Draglen Brothers series. Loved it! This book had everything: Hot dragons, lovers' turmoil, passion, a quick wedding, a new baby, and a mother's wrath. I loved how he had decided and was willing to give up everything to be with her. Both of them were so afraid of getting hurt they almost messed up their chance at love. I loved it when Marilyn had the baby and Hawken and Fewton couldn't handle it. I literally laughed out loud and had to read that section to my daughter because she wanted to know what was so funny. I can't wait to read the next one.

BETA 5, 5 stars, I absolutely loved this book. I have enjoyed each and every one of The Draglen Brothers and their stories, but I like Layern the best. He is absolutely in my opinion the freakiest of the brothers. If you have read Draken and Showken then you know that's saying a lot. You can tell almost from the beginning that he is going to fall head over heels for Reseda, even though the poor girl tries to ignore and dismiss his advances. He just never gives up. I loved Reseda's character, she is such a strong woman even though you can tell she carries a lot of pain and anger due to the situation the Queen (who also happens to be Layern's mother) has put her and her family into. All through the story I was guessing and speculating about why the Queen would have banned her and punished her mother who was once the Queens best friend. But when all was revealed, all I could think was huh, didn't see that coming. The relationship between Layern and Reseda was explosive almost from the beginning. I was starting to think that poor girl was going to need an underwear allowance lol. I loved how when the shit hit the fan, the Draglen brothers and their wives as well as one much unsuspected person rallied around Layern and Reseda. I couldn't help but wonder if, between Reseda's jealous best friend, his crazy "witch" of a cousin and Layern's vengeful mother, these two would get their happily ever after. This story held my attention from start to finish, and in my opinion is the best out of all the Draglen Brothers. I would strongly recommended this book to anyone, especially if you are a fan of Paranormal and erotic stories, then this is the book for you.

GLOSSARY

Afla (n) – means ass or butt.

Aumdo (n) - The Laws, written in book form for dragons.

Brocur (n) – nephew.

Cortamagen (n) - The land where the Draglen brothers live.

Conete (v) – Marry.

Cati (adj) - Foolish, silly.

Dorli (ejac) - I apologize.

Drangrands (n) – Grandparents.

Envo (n) – Draglen Family Throne.

Giver (n) - A man or woman chosen by one of the Draglen Descendants to fulfill his or her sexual needs; the position approximates to that of a kept mistress.

Homla (n) – Mom or Mother.

Hulin (n) - A cliff that belongs to Draglen Dragons.

Joha (n) – The gift of knowing the future.

Kalin (n) - The planet on which Cortamagen is located.

Key (n) -A human who keeps a portal open for dragons to travel from his or her land to Earth. Not all humans have this ability.

Ki (v) – sexual dreams.

Leka (n) - A loyal friend.

Lecena (n) – A beautiful flower.

Magen (n) - The language of Cortamagen.

Malekse (n)- the news giver.

Meech (v) – Means to eat and talk.

Merr (v)- to vanish.

Molla (n) - The male mate in Kalin.

Noke (n) – The land near Cortamagen.

Sio (v) - to forgive.

Siscur (n) – Niece.

Taker (n) - A dragon who has taken a Giver.

Wella (n) -The female mate in Kalin.

Youngs (n) -Children.

Zell (n) - Beloved.

MY LOVE

I was determined to have you my love.

Determined to show you I could be gentle as a dove,

I knew that we would fit like a glove.

OH YES! My love.

You consumed me, yes, only you, never knew I would find a fire

like you,

But, OH yes,

You give me such desire

My love my body aches when I'm away from you,

My life would be void if not for you.

OH YES

My joy. My peace. My Wella!

MY LOVE.

By Solease M Barner.

LAYERN

I should never have put my life on hold for her. Now that I'm back
to myself, I'm catching up with as many females as I can. Five
years, shit, I will never go that long without sex again. I love sex.
It's the best part of life. I've always had the upper hand with a
female I take to bed. Now that Showken has a Wella, he can't go
on the hunt with me for new women, so I have enlisted Gemi and
Fewton. They are always happy to please females. I'm glad we are
taking a break from Earth. Father wants all the family around
Marilyn, since she's carrying the first Draglen descendent for the
next generation. He's very cautious about things of this nature. I'm
sure Cess will be with young soon, also. Well, I have been waiting
for Gemi and Fewton for a few minutes now. We are flying to a
neighboring land, Noke. It's filled with beautiful female dragon-
shifters, plus it's where Maka lives. She and I were in love, or I
was in love with her. I wanted her to be my Wella until I found she

had been with another dragon-shifter. After killing him, I could not stand to look at her. I took a vow of celibacy until my love no longer belonged to her. I'm hoping to let her see how happy I can be without her. I look over my shoulder, and spot Gemi and Fewton.

"What took so long?" I ask, studying them. I'm the brother you can't lie to. I would know. Though I don't know for certain if they are lying, I'm usually right. The gift I have is hard to explain, I received it from my mother's side of the family. My gift is not as strong as Mother's. I can't predict the future as well as she can, but feelings and thoughts, I'm pretty good with those, especially with dragons. Humans are more complex at times, but over time I break down what they are hiding, too.

"Gemi," Fewton says, "I just finished playing with some of the servants." As they reach me, I feel myself getting excited. Lately, I can't stop myself from wanting female company. I really deprived myself far too long.

"Well, I'm ready to change into our dragons so we can go," I say. My brothers nod in agreement and we spread out to give ourselves room as we change. My dragon is blue, Mother says because I have the gift of joha, or moods of knowing. We all change and fly to Noke.

***

Making it there in good time, we transform back into human form, in a field that's reserved for just the Draglen family. The servants are there waiting with wraps for us.

"Ok, brothers," I say, sniffing the air. "I'm pretty sure I hear music, which means sexy dancing dragon females. It also seems, we have a few other species out to play, mermaids and fairies." I smile, remembering how much fun they can be.

"Layern," Gemi says. "I'm glad you are back. I thought you would stay celibate." Fewton is too busy walking towards the music even to think about what we are saying. Fewton loves women just as much as I do. Gemi likes to please them, but he wants a Wella. The music gets louder and I can hear the singing. This is going to be a fun night. Fewton has found a few females to play with. Gemi looks at me.

"I'll see you in the morning?" he asks. I smile, nodding, glancing about the area for my play toys for the night. None of us currently has a Giver. We like variety, but sometimes we take a Giver just not to have to seduce. Gemi heads over to the garden, where a group is drinking and dancing. I'm one of the best dancers among my brothers. Making a female of any species orgasm during dancing is pleasurable for me. I see a couple of dragons eyeing me. I can even hear them speaking about me. "Prince Layern is here," one says. "Prince Layern, just to have one night..." I walk their way. I can make their dream a reality.

"Hello, Lecenas," I say. Lecena means flower. In Kalin it's a great compliment to call a female a flower. They both smile, I pull them to the middle of the dancing arena. Their bodies are twisting, turning, and grinding on one another. The music is so sensual and sexy. The dragon females begin to dance with me. I squeeze the hips of the one with the golden eyes as I pull her closer. The other one, who has pink eyes, has her back against me as she dances, sliding up and down my body. We get a rhythm going and they are mush in my hands.

I'm able to touch them any place I want. We kiss as we dance. I'm having fun when I spot a woman with red hair staring at me with piercing light orange eyes. She's a dragon, but not all the way. How can that be? The only half dragon is in Marilyn's stomach. The law allowing the birth of half dragons has only been approved in the last hundred years, where did she come from? I have never seen her before. She walks with such grace and class. You would think she was royalty. I would have known this, though. We know all the other royal families on this planet. I can no longer focus on the dragon women I'm dancing with. I must know who this dragon is! I let my gift seek for her, yet even though we are making eye contact, my gift is blocked. She smiles as if she knows. I give each of the dragons a kiss, and walk straight for her.

"Hello."

"Hello," she says back.

"Your name, please?" I ask.

"Prince Layern, I know who you are. You should know who I am." I hear the hurt in her voice. This woman is a mystery. I narrow my eyes. I don't like playing guessing games.

"You know who I am, good, then tell me your name." She stares directly at me. We don't blink. She takes a deep breath, and gives me a smile.

"My name is Reseda, and I'm dragon and human, the first of my kind." She speaks with pride. I know this cannot be true.

"Reseda, you lie," I snap. "The first of that kind will be born to my brother's Wella," I never get pissed, but her telling such a lie is disrespectful. I'm not sure what kind of magic she's playing with, but I do smell human cells within her body.

"I only speak the truth, you should ask Queen Nala who I am. She knows, as she banned me from Kalin," she says, looking into my eyes. I'm thrown back by her beauty. Her skin is flawless, her body is perfect and she's offended me.

"Keep the Queen, my mother, out of your speech," I say. "If she knew you spoke with such disrespect, she would have your head." This Reseda has me angry and aroused at the same time. I really want to lick her pretty skin. She looks and smells amazing.

"I don't care about your queen," she snaps, "as far as I can tell, she's an evil dragon." Who the hell is this?

"Reseda," I say, stepping closer, "I'm not sure how many passes I can give you, with that tongue of yours. You know I'm willing to overlook everything you said, and allow you to make it up to me with that venomous tongue you have, all over my body." We are now only about an inch apart. I hear her heart beating faster. She looks a little shaken at what I have just said.

"How dare you?"

"I do dare, do you accept?"

"No, you need to walk away from me." She glares, and her eyes flicker. She's a dragon, alright.

"Reseda, this is getting serious, I came to Noke to find a dragon for the night, to please her, everywhere. Would you like that?" I ask, sliding my hands around her waist. I start moving her body with the beat of the music. She rolls her eyes, and begins to dance with me. I can't believe how good a dancer she is. Her body is all over me, I feel my sex rising as she brings a leg around my waist, holding me as she climbs my body, twisting her body sensually. She throws her head back, letting the dancing, not her mind, control her body. I find myself wanting her now. I run my hands up her body, letting her lead. She leans back as she lets her body continue the lovely moves. I smile, knowing she will be in a bed with me tonight. The music stops. She slides down my body. I look her in the eyes as she tries to come out of my hold.

"I have to go. My time is up." She pushes harder against me, and I squeeze tighter.

"No, I like our time together, and I would like to continue to have more time with you in private."

"You don't understand, I have no choice, I sneaked into Kalin. My time is limited before Queen Nala senses my presence."

"Reseda, you need to explain."

"Listen, I thought I could hate you, but I see now you don't know about me. You really don't want me, I'm not human, not dragon, in between species." She looks around. I keep my eyes on her, though. "I have to go, it's nice to meet one of the Draglen brothers, and I've only heard stories about you from my mother."

"Who is your mother?" I ask.

"She's the reason I sneak into Noke. My mother is nothing but a servant now, but at one time, she and the queen were best friends."

"Reseda, this story you tell is getting even more outrageous. Come, I have a place where we can talk and sleep," I say.

"Please let me go, I'm not what you think, and I will not do what you want."

"I'll let you go, Reseda, but you must promise to contact me when you come again." I lean to kiss her, and she turns her head.

"Ok, no kiss, then. How old are you?"

"On Earth, I'm twenty-four years old; really I'm three hundred and ten years old. Now, I have to go," she pleads.

I release her and then she turns, running in a full sprint, not as fast as dragons but still very fast. Eventually she disappears into the night. I stand there a minute, wondering what just happened. I came here to have sex with some hot dragons, but now I have to get some answers. Reseda does have human blood, but she is dragon too. Her eyes changed in front of me from human to her beast. 'Reseda, you are not going to get rid of me like that,' I say in my thoughts. I can't figure it out tonight. I glance over my shoulder and see the two dragon women staring at me, still hoping. I walk over to them.

"I would like to have you both, can I?" I ask. I already know they are willing to do anything to say they have had sex with a Draglen brother.

"Yes, we accept your offer, Prince Layern, and may we say it's our pleasure to be with you, and an honor," the one with the pink eyes says. I smile. Taking both their hands, I lead them away to my place for the night. I will lose myself with these beauties for tonight, and in the morning I will go in search of Reseda. She will not get off that easily.

RESEDA

I'm so dead. What was I thinking? I should have run the other way when I saw it was a Draglen brother. My curiosity got the better of me. Well, and I'm pissed off at Queen Nala also. I need to learn to use my head, and not let my temper get in the way. I'm sure he has already told the Queen. It's just a matter of time before she hunts me down and rips me apart. I got out as fast as I could after having the best dance ever with Prince Layern. He is a fantastic dancer. I can't believe how attractive he is. I mean, I've seen pictures of the brothers, but never in real life. Those deep blue eyes with that soft dark brown hair, gosh he even smelled heavenly. I finally make it back to my home in New Orleans, Louisiana. I have one of the best homes in the historic parts of the city. My home is beautiful. It's surrounded by black wrought-iron gates. I have five bedrooms and three baths. I've recently made a friend named Palmer; he's pretty friendly. He doesn't suspect me to be anything but a human.

Palmer is a good friend, but I think he secretly likes me. I can't even see him as more than a friend. I walk into my mini library and take a seat on my soft white lounge chair. Leaning my head back, I smile, thinking about how I met a Draglen brother tonight, and of all the brothers, the one all the women in Noke talk about at that. Prince Layern, wow! I even got a chance to dance with him. I have never danced like that. I felt so comfortable with him. Now that I have opened my mouth, I have to stay away for a while. Queen Nala, according to my mother, will rip me into pieces. If I ever get a chance to meet her, I'll tell her how evil she is, even if it costs me my life. I feel myself getting sleepy, so I curl up into a ball. Smiling about my dance with Prince Layern, I drift off to sleep.

***

"Reseda, Reseda!" I hear my name being yelled, but I'm sure it's way too early for company, and this is my lazy day. The knocking at the door does not stop. I squeeze my eyes tight, trying to ignore my name.

"RESEDA!" My name is yelled again. Taking a deep breath, I smell him instantly, oh the joys of being half dragon. I walk slowly to the door, remembering I'm still in my clothes from last night, including heels, I always change back into my human clothes once I return to Earth. I pull the door open, rolling my eyes.

"Palmer, it's too early for company, you need a girlfriend so you won't bother me so much." I wave him inside as I walk towards the kitchen. I need coffee and food.

"You know I'm waiting for you to fall for me, Reseda."

"Ha ha, Palmer, remember I told you that all I want is a friend?" I say. I start the coffee pot and move to the fridge, pulling out eggs, butter, cheese, onion, bacon and my pre-made fruit bowl.

"Yes, I know what you told me, but a man has to try, right?"

"How often are you going to try?"

"I always try once a week, maybe one day you will say yes,"

"Please stop wasting your time on me... I'm not who you think I am," I say, looking him in the eyes, pleading with him to stop pursuing me and just be my friend.

"I'm not trying to make you uncomfortable. You know I will always be your friend," Palmer smiles. "I came by your house last night to see if you wanted to go to hear some blues with me, but I got no answer."

I look over my shoulder as I place the bacon in the skillet, wondering. Do friends ask these sorts of questions?

"Yeah, I was out pretty late last night."

"I guess so. You're still in the clothes I saw you in yesterday morning."

"Friend-"

"Ok, ok, what do you have planned today?" I frown to myself, wishing I didn't have to be so secretive with Palmer. I would love nothing more than to say to him, just once, 'I'm half dragon and was thrown off my native land, but I occasionally sneak back in to see my mother who is a full dragon but can be in human form.' I start cracking eggs into a mixing bowl, adding salt and pepper. Then I move to the onion to chop up a handful for my eggs. I stop and notice Palmer is just staring at me, with those 'I want to fuck you' eyes. I sigh very loudly.

"Stop staring at me like that," I shout, "or I will ask you to leave, Palmer!" I can't ever get his hopes up about me, I'm a dragon.

"Shit, Reseda, you take things so serious, I get it, friend, but I can stare and dream. Fuck, I'm a man." He raises his brows at me, smiling.

"I'm sorry, Palmer, I know you are a man, just don't want you to wait for me, but it's no excuse to be rude, and for that I apologize." I bite my lip, hoping he accepts.

"Reseda, who could be angry with you for just being honest, now back to my question. What do you have planned for today?"

"I'm staying at home and being lazy: movies, food and sleep. I'm very tired," I say. Every time I travel through the portal it makes me very tired and hungry. I feel like I'm leaving my true home. I know I'm half human, but the dominant gene is dragon. I just wish I could stay in Kalin forever.

"Well, I could watch a movie with you. Then I got some family business, but I want to go dancing tonight in the Bayou. Are you up for that?"

I smile, remembering my dance with Prince Layern. Now, no dancing I do will ever be enough. I remove the bacon from the skillet, and start on my eggs.

"If I say no, you will still stop by and bug me to go. So, I guess I'm going dancing tonight, but let the record show, I did just want to have a lazy day."

"Darling, it's just a little past eight in the morning, you can be lazy all you want, besides, the breakfast you're making is going to make you lie around." He smiles. Palmer was shocked at how much I could eat when we first became friends. I told him dancing helps me keep my figure, but being part dragon my appetite is huge and I'm always frustrated, given that I've only had sex maybe twenty times out of the entire three hundred and ten years of my life. I narrow my eyes at him with a slight smile.

After finishing my breakfast, I need to shower and get comfy with a movie and some sweet tea. I tell Palmer to go find a movie while I take a quick shower, and I will be down in a flash. Standing in the shower, letting the warm water run over my body, I can't help but think about how Prince Layern would feel again, his warm hands running over my body like the dance we shared. I haven't contacted my mother yet, but I will soon. I will have to stay away and hope Queen Nala doesn't find out, DAMN! I should have kept my mouth closed. Those blue eyes had me in a cage. I should have resisted him. I was not thinking at all. Remembering Palmer is downstairs I finish my shower, and get dressed in some comfy clothes. Looking in the mirror, I notice my hair has grown some; I brush it out and decide to let it air dry. It will still be beautiful, since I inherited my mother's beautiful hair. I walk into my den and find Palmer looking at some of my books on the wall.

"Palmer, you know you're not a big reader, why are you looking at my books?" I say.

"How did you get these first editions of some of these books? I mean they are almost three hundred years old, even older," Palmer says. "You have some first editions of Charles Dickens' books, I may not read often, but I do know something about antiques." He glances at me, but I give nothing away. Keeping my face undisturbed, I smile.

"You know I come from a family with money, but it's no big deal. Now, what movie did you pick?" I say, smiling. I brush off this conversation. I'm three hundred and ten, I was around when they were published, and they're nothing but old books to me. He sighs, but decides to come join me on the sofa. I smile, relieved that he has dropped the subject. I have books that museums would kill for.

"I thought we could start out with some action and watch 'The Wolverine'. I hear it was a good movie."

"Sounds good, push play."

I get up and go get the pitcher of sweet tea and two glasses. I decide to bring a bag of cashews, also.

The movie starts and Palmer is excited, but all I can think about is how I'm so much like Wolverine. I'm something different, and don't fit. My father always had to explain odd things I did, until I could control my dragon. I remember when I first realized I could breathe fire. Needless to say, I destroyed an entire village in South America. That day still haunts me, all those people, luckily the fatalities were minimal. I force myself to lock that memory back up and enjoy the movie with Palmer. We watch the movie in silence with our sweet tea and our nuts.

***

The day goes by slowly after Palmer leaves, but after a few movies, lunch and a nap, it is time to get ready for my evening with Palmer. Palmer wants to go dancing. He and I are pretty good at dancing together, but after dancing with Prince Layern I'm not sure how I'm going to dance with another man without fantasizing over him. I stand inside my closet, trying to pick the best outfit to dance in and still be sexy. I glance at my dresses and notice a short, loose, sleeveless, light blue dress, with a high enough split on the left to give my leg room as I dance. This dress is perfect, now all I need is my heels and just a few items, and I will be ready. I lay my clothes on the bed with my lace panties. I always feel good in lace. I decide to have another shower. After spending the day eating, sleeping and watching movies, a shower is needed. I don't want to smell like snacks.

After my shower, I wrap a towel around my body and turn some music on my stereo system, blasting Maroon 5. I can't help dancing back to the bathroom, my mind drifts back to Layern's touch on my hips. I close my eyes, as my body twists and turns. Oh, I wish I could live in my birth land and be free, or at least welcome, to travel back and forth without fearing death from

Queen Nala. My mood instantly changes for the worse, and my eyes fill with tears. I miss my dad so much, he would know what to say to me. Now, I'm left alone to figure all this out for myself. I shake off that feeling and turn on the blow dryer, enjoying the shine in my hair as it dries. I love my red hair, it really reflects my personality. Glancing at the clock and seeing it's a little past nine p.m., I pick up my pace and get ready.

As I am doing a last spin in front of the mirror, the doorbell rings. I walk down the stairs, opening the door to see Palmer looking handsome.

"Damn, woman, you look good! I think you should give me a chance," Palmer says, smiling.

"Palmer, you have just cost yourself the first dance, and please stop asking to have a chance with me. I love you as a friend, ok?"

"Ok, can I have my first dance back?"

"NO!" I say. After locking the door, I jump in the car with Palmer. I feel like dancing, maybe I might meet someone worthy to take home. This will be a fun night.

LAYERN

"Did you find her?" I ask Hawken.

"Yes, but Layern, I have a bad feeling about this, and you're the one with the gift."

"Hawken, don't worry. I will not go alone. Gemi is going with me, but I need to find out if what she says is true."

I smile to myself, I can't get this beautiful redhead out of my mind. I have a strong need to see her again, and besides, she ran from me. Women don't run from me. They always run to me.

"Layern, if she is right and Queen Nala, our mother, banned her, I think you would be wise to step away from this quest."

"I'm taking the voice of reason with me, Gemi," I say calmly, "and brother... if it's true what she says, we should know more about her, and why she's banned. Now, hand over all the information you have on her, including her current address."

"This could end badly," he says. He hands me the stack of

papers on Reseda. I can't wait to smell her again. As I turn to leave, I feel Hawken's intentions.

"You should not do that." We stare at each other for less than 30 seconds, but long enough for me to send him a visual picture of the damage I will do to him if he opens his mouth.

"FUCK YOU!"

"I love you too, now I have to go." I turn my back, ending the conversation. I can still feel the anger steaming off Hawken. I know he can't help being the malekse. Sometimes I think he doesn't even resist the urge. I forget these thoughts without hesitation, for there's a certain half-breed who ran from me, and said no. I must see her again.

After a good two hours, I find Gemi in the castle library, writing. Gemi is very frustrated in his life right now. I wish my brother would find love.

"Brother, you still up for going back to Earth with me?"

"To find the human? Layern, we are not to leave, because our new sister is with Young."

Damn, that will surely get fire blowing, but I can't stop thinking I have to find her. I'll take the chance.

"Yes, to find the human. Brother, what if she is dragon too? I think we should find out more."

"I think you want more of her."

"That too, but I promise that finding her attractive will not keep me from finding out the truth, ok?"

"Fine but if…"

"I already know, you will make me come back, with no hesitation."

"Sometimes, you should stay out of people's feelings."

"If only it were that easy. Let's leave tonight."

"Why not right now?"

"Two reasons, first, I have a date in an hour," I grin. "Second, less chance of being caught by our mother."

"Ok, just remember what you promised."

"Gemi, no worries, I think it will do you good."

Gemi glares at me with a low growl. I know he hates that I know so much about what he wants, but I never share with any of the others. Brumen and Fewton would have a laugh about his thoughts. Warton, well let's just say he doesn't care about anything except winning a fight, war, or argument. The others are so busy, except Beauka. She's starting to get jealous because of not being the only princess in the palace, although she would never admit it, and would try to rip my head off if I ever spoke this out loud.

"Ok, we leave tonight, we can meet at my pond."

"Thanks, brother, see you at sunset."

It's settled. Tonight I will get a chance to see the mysterious Reseda. I look at the stack of papers I have to read about her, but I have to make up for years of going without sex. Maybe I will get a chance with Reseda, right now Ki will more than satisfy my sexual needs. I take the papers to my room, and head out for a little fun.

***

I walk to Gemi's pond. He is sitting on the edge, ready. I love my brother. He is often misunderstood, but he is the voice of reason among us all.

"You ready?"

"Yes, I'm ready. I hate the fact clothes are always such a need on Earth."

"Gemi, where we are going, you will like it." I smile, pulling out my hand portal.

"Layern, where are we going?"

I was able to find time to read all the information on Reseda. The only thing Hawken could find was her life on Earth. He found nothing that said she had even been to Kalin.

"The south, just follow me," I say. We both pull out our portals, take one glance and jump in.

After a few minutes, we are standing in front of Reseda's home. Gemi turns to me.

"Layern, she lives in the French Quarter in New Orleans?"

"Yes she does, but she's not home," I say. I notice Gemi is staring at me. "What?"

"I really hope you know what you're doing, she could be trouble."

"I know," I say "I like trouble, let's have a look inside her home." I turn to see if someone is watching us, but I see no one, yet I feel a presence. My beast instantly searches through the darkness, and the presence leaves. Gemi's beast is on guard as well.

"Do you think we have visitors?" Gemi glares into the darkness.

"If we do, they will not approach, come."

We transport instantly into the house, and I can smell her everywhere. I smile, as the scent is intoxicating. Gemi goes to her kitchen and finds food. I run up the stairs, looking for her bedroom. I walk up to a door that is painted all black. I walk in and see her bed arranged to where she can see the sky as she sleeps. Her sheets look as if she hasn't slept. I walk over and take a deep breath. "She sleeps here sometimes," I say out loud. I walk over to her bathroom and pick up her towel from the floor, raising it to my nose. "Mmmm." I inhale deeply. She has a unique smell, it's a combination of lilac and coconut. I glance at her luxurious bathroom. She seems to love the Victorian style. I walk out, and into a very modern closet for this home. This was an update. I open a couple of drawers until I come to her underwear. Everything is so neat. I walk out of the room and after I finish looking upstairs, I find Gemi in her library, she has a T.V. in this room. I shake my head, not understanding the meaning of placing a library and T.V. in the same room. I sniff the air, picking up another scent. A man. A man who spends time with her in this room. Gemi is looking at her books.

"Layern, she has books she shouldn't have." I snap out of my search to see if I can smell sex in the room.

"What books are you talking about?" I ask. I walk over and

see books from our land, things like our history, language, even a map of places in Kalin.

"I think we should leave this girl alone. If Mother banned her, I don't want to be around when she finds out we are seeking someone she clearly hates." Gemi glares. He's angry. No one ever wants to be on the bad side of the queen, but she is our mother. She would only do so much harm to her sons.

"Brother, listen… why would our mother be threatened by her? If she is dangerous, I want to know if we should allow her access back into Kalin. We have to check this out."

"NO, we don't!" he snaps. "We should go."

"I want to find her, ask her some questions."

"No, no we should go. Layern, let it go. She has a punishment on her head from our mother, we should go."

"I'm not leaving, if you want to leave, go. I'm going to search her out in the city."

We growl at each other. The problem with being a dragon-shifter is that when the human side is upset, the beast can become fierce.

"If I stay with you, it's only to keep you under control."

"Don't worry, Mother is too busy preparing for her very first Grand Young, she has no time for us." I say. "I know her scent well, it should not take long to find her."

He nods as he follows me. Her scent leads me to a nightclub where people are dancing, eating and having a good time. I like it already. I glance and see Gemi is smiling.

"I'll find her, you have a good time, brother."

"I always try" he says, smiling.

Gemi walks right into the crowd, holding the women's attention. I hear the whispers around me. The women, and even a few men, are wondering who I am. I know Reseda is here. Her smell is very intense. My eyes roam over the people until I spot her dancing with a guy. My movements are determined as I keep my eyes on her. I send Gemi a mental message that I have found her. I get a reply from him to give him a minute. She stops dancing, although the music is still playing and the people are still dancing. Her back is to me. Why has she stopped? The male is asking her what is wrong. Then it hits me: if she's part dragon, she senses me. She slowly turns around, and our eyes lock. I keep walking until I finally reach her, stopping just a foot away.

"Hello Reseda, can I have a dance?" I ask. Her male friend does not seem pleased to see me.

"She came here with me, go find someone else to dance with," he snaps.

I smile at Reseda, not breaking eye contact with her. She is just staring at me. I was hoping she would be happy to see me, but she looks as if she has seen a ghost.

"Hey, buddy, you need to leave, she doesn't want to dance with you," the man says. He steps closer to me. My eyes leave hers, and I see a pair of angry eyes looking at me. I narrow my eyes, knowing this is the guy who has been in her house. He doesn't even know the truth about her. I will not hurt this man, but

I have been thinking about her ever since she disappeared in the woods in Noke. I'm not backing down. I look behind him, watching Gemi coming through the crowd towards us. We are never to make a scene in public. Reseda finds her voice after a few deep breaths.

"It's ok, Palmer," she says nervously, "I know him, he's… an old friend." He has a name, Palmer. Oh, he likes her.

"I'm not leaving, you look frightened." Palmer reaches for her hand and I growl very low. He looks up at me.

"Palmer," I say, calmly, "my patience is running out, and my brother has no patience." He turns and sees Gemi standing behind him. People are starting to take notice. I hold out my hand for her, and very slowly she places it in mine.

"I'm not sure who you are," Palmer snaps, "but I'm not afraid of you." I ignore his statement, he would be more careful with his words if he knew who I was. He walks angrily off the dance floor.

A new song starts, and I pull Reseda close and start a slow, sensual dance, staring into her beautiful grey eyes.

"How did you find me?" she asks. I smile a little. I look her in the eyes for a moment, and I keep getting bits and pieces of her feelings, it's very frustrating.

"Reseda, you caught my interest and when you ran… well, I am a predator."

"You are going to get my mother and me killed," she snaps. Her eyes narrow, and for a moment her beast is revealed with a low growl from her chest. I really like her.

"You should relax and just dance with me and my brother," I say. I send Gemi a message to come join us.

"I'm dancing with you, Prince Layern, but Queen Nala hates me, and this is not safe."

"Why? and please call me Layern."

"Why what?"

"Why does she hate you?" Gemi arrives just as the music changes to a song which is unfamiliar, yet it makes my body really want to dance. My hips circle up against hers and she meets me with every twist. A smile comes across her face as she starts really feeling the music. Gemi holds her hips and begins dancing with her from behind, while I handle her front. I can see other dancers looking as they dance. Dancing is in our DNA, but I have yet to meet one better at any dancing than me. I pull my shirt over my head as we both forget the conversation that we started. I make sure to keep eye contact as I dance up and down her body. I reach her face and slowly lick across her lower lip, and I feel her mood change to sexual. I look and see her friend Palmer, staring daggers at me. I laugh out loud. The dance is very intense as Gemi grabs her beautiful shoulder-length red hair and pulls her head back, and I hear the moan escape, 'ahhh' is the sound. The dance doesn't stop. Our sensual movements give me the opportunity I need. I slide my hands down her body, memorizing her scent, but I have plans to keep that scent with me. This time as I slide down her body, my face is in perfect position to place a kiss on her pelvic bone. Not letting this chance pass me by, I lean forward and pull her to me, pressing a kiss through her dress. I wish I could feel her emotions, but her body is responding splendidly, I hear my brother whispering sweet things in her ear to keep her calm about being in public, while I make my move.

My hands slide up her dress, reaching a lace thong. I smile to myself, for it is perfect. I feel her legs tense, but my romantic brother has her covered. Reseda relaxes as my hands slide across her warm vagina. I rub softly as my hands find her hips, and my index finger finds the band of her panties, teasing her a little. I hear Gemi keeping her calm. I pull the panties and they tear at both sides- just what I wanted. I bunch the front of them in my hand and begin to pull them between her legs, making sure to hit her clitoris with each movement. I finally have them in my hand, and a great wave of pleasure runs through my body. I dance back up her body, sliding her panties into my pocket. The expression on her face is a mixture of excitement and fear. I smile and lean in, giving her a surprise kiss. I think she's so in shock she can't say anything. I smile slightly. I continue to dance, and my brother leaves to find a little fun with human women.

"Reseda, you ok?" I ask. I place my head very close to her ear, but not because she cannot hear me. She has dragon blood, so her hearing is fantastic. I just want the sexual connection to stay. I hear her heartbeat go from fast to extreme.

"I'm not sure, I..." I place a soft kiss on her shoulder. I would usually be more discreet on Earth, but she is lovely. I hear the song 'Bad', by Wale. I keep up with music from both planets, I'm the best dancer, and can dance to anything.

"Can we go somewhere to talk?" I ask. I hope she says yes, I really would like to be inside her. I feel caged around her, I'm sure when I'm inside her this feeling of need will leave.

"I don't want to talk with you," she whispers "besides, you have my panties, can I have them back?"

"No, they are mine now. You let me take them," I say, smiling.

RESEDA

I can't believe he is smiling about taking my panties. I feel so ashamed, my father would not be happy, but damn, Prince Layern has my panties in his pocket. That's sexy as hell.

"I had no choice," I frown. "Prince Gemi was saying such lustful words, and your hands were up my dress." I close my eyes, trying to stop the need to orgasm right here on the dance floor.

"I really need to talk with you. The last time I saw you, you had some very profound things to say about my mother. I want to know more."

"NO!" I say. "I'm not talking with you. I said too much already." I walk away from the floor. I feel him right behind me. Palmer is coming towards me. I shake my head. I don't want him getting hurt. The Draglen Brothers have a reputation for getting aggressive if need be. I see the sign that says WOMEN, and walk into the bathroom. I take a deep breath. I feel safe in the lavatory. I walk into one of the stalls, feeling completely naked without my panties on. I start remembering his hands, oh my, he kissed my pelvic bone. Why is he here? I can still sense him outside the bathroom. Damn, Prince Layern is here, with my panties in his pocket. Oh, ohhh, he wants me, no... what else could it be? He does have my panties in his pocket, wait, I'm not into having a threesome, though, and I have never really had a great sexual experience. I can't, he will be disappointed, and to be with a Draglen Brother is an honor. My body feels like a roller coaster right now. I need to have a release. It's been so long. I stand still, remembering his words, his lips on mine, the pulling of my panties, and I just explode with my orgasm running down my legs, I scream out in pleasure. I just let it go, and for the first time, I feel sexual relief. How can this be from just a dance? Well, a sexual dance, but even with that I'm not thinking. I have to get away from Prince Layern, my mother's life depends on it. If I have to face Queen Nala I will, but my mother is weak and I have no strength to fight with Queen Nala. I pull some tissue and wipe my inner thighs and my sex. It's dripping in my juice. I have never felt this good and exhausted. If I walk out of the bathroom he will be there waiting. I'm so wrapped up in my thoughts that I am too late to use a portal to leave when I hear some women speaking.

"Damn, you in the ladies' room, baby, but I don't mind," one drunk lady says.

"Shit, are you looking for me, if you're not, I'm looking for you," another one says.

I hold my breath, because I can smell Prince Layern in the ladies' bathroom.

"Reseda, I know what just happened, and I can help you out more," he says.

"Please get out of the ladies' bathroom. You know it's illegal to be in here," I say, hoping he leaves. I hear one of the women say, "He can stay if I can touch his chest, DAMN!" I shake my head. These women are so consumed with lust. They are not aware of the beast inside him. I open the stall, bumping right into him.

"There you are, you ready to talk?" Layern says, smiling. I want my panties back, and that smile off his face. He heard me orgasm in the bathroom, I feel so embarrassed.

"Leave me alone, please."

"Sorry, I can't. I need answers, along with other things. I think you do, too, Reseda Fire."

He knows my birth name, oh shit. This is not happening, what does he want? Well, I know he wants sex, but what is this talking he wants to do? Unless it's a lie. I have to get out of here. I walk over to the faucet to wash my hands. I have heard Prince Layern has the gift of experiencing other people's feelings. I'm not sure if he can feel mine. My mother and father had me hide myself so much, and I'm used to being a puzzle. I see him watching my every move. I see the ladies walk out of the bathroom, and before he can get close enough, I pull my portal out of my purse and disappear.

I go straight to Palmer's house. I know he's angry with me,

but this is the one place that Prince Layern won't look for me. I don't even know how to explain anything to Palmer, he's my friend, but tonight I hurt him, and now I'm asking for a safe place. I knock on the door. I hear him walking inside the house and then I hear him at the door, but he doesn't open it.

"What?" Oh, he is really mad.

"Palmer," I say nervously, "I'm sorry, it's just, I mean they… I can't say." I can't tell Palmer anything. I feel like a horrible friend, but I'm not sure about the Draglen Brothers. By what I have been told and what I have read, they are deadly. I hear the door unlock and open. Palmer is standing there, wearing nothing but a pair of jeans, with a very angry look in his brown eyes. He looks handsome, and he will make someone happy one day. He waves me in, and I walk cautiously in, hoping to save our friendship. A gust of warm wind blows under my dress, reminding me of my lack of underwear. I would be more comfortable if I were in Noke, but I'm not.

"I need to explain some things, but you will have to understand there will be things I just can't tell you."

"Bullshit! It's some things you don't want to tell me." He takes a deep breath. "You know I have been trying to be more than just a friend since we met, and yet you let a stranger come up to you in the club, and touch you more than I ever have. You owe me an explanation."

"First, I owe you nothing, understand? I told you when we met that we could be nothing but friends, and Pri… Layern is not a stranger, and it's complicated. I still want us to be friends, but I need you not to ask questions about him or his brother."

"Oh, that was his brother who was feeling you up from behind! I could have killed them both." I see the pain in Palmer's eyes. I have never led him on, and did he think if he stayed around I would just give in? That could never happen, I'm part dragon.

"I just stopped by to say I'm sorry." I say, "I need to go home. There are a lot of things that I must think about." I am turning to leave when Palmer turns me around, and before I can think, his lips are on mine. It's soft and sweet, but I feel nothing but more pain now.

"I love you, Reseda, just give us a try. I would be good to you."

I close my eyes, knowing that what I say next will be the most difficult thing I will ever do.

"Palmer, I love you, but only as a friend. I'm not sexually attracted to you. It has nothing to do with you. You're a very nice - looking guy and will make a woman happy one day, it just won't be me."

He raises his hand and gently rubs my cheek.

"Reseda, you are a beautiful woman, I hope you will change your mind one day." I say nothing. I walk out the door, down his stairs, and start for home. I don't want to hear any more of his love for me, especially knowing Prince Layern has shown me some interest. I'm not sure if he just wants sex or something else. I just know that this is the best I've ever felt in my entire miserable, confined, secretive life.

I walk home, which is only about six blocks away. If it were anyone else I would say it was dangerous to walk alone at night, but I'm not afraid of anyone. I'm the one who could do the damage. My mind is going a hundred miles an hour trying to figure out why Prince Layern is seeking me out. He even stole my panties and heard my orgasm in the bathroom, very embarrassing. I continue to walk, passing the beautiful houses, listening to the dogs bark and then back away. I have never been able to have a pet, I tried once and I got angry and it turned out really bad.

I stop to just look up into the sky,that is when I smell another dragon, shit, Prince Layern. How? I pick up my pace and try to behave normally, but I know he can be in front of me if he so chooses. I finally make it to my block and clearly see my home, I just need to get inside. I can't deal with his sexual advances, I could have had sex with him on the dance floor. He has the ability to make you forget about the other people around. I reach my gate, and that's when I hear my name.

"Reseda, you did right by Palmer, you and he could never work."

I felt bad already, I don't need to hear that, even if it's the truth. "Fuck you," I say, and run up the porch, only to find myself standing next to Layern. This is not happening.

LAYERN

"Reseda, Reseda," I say smiling, "you must stop running from me. I will always be able to smell you."

"Prince Layern-"

"Layern, just Layern to you."

"You have to stay away from me," she yells. "Queen Nala would have my head. My mother would be the first to make me suffer for disobeying." She stands against the door, holding the knob. I place my hand over hers, keeping her from escaping into her home.

"Listen, stop worrying about my mother, I know you want me. You are good at keeping your feelings away from me, but I smell your arousal all around me, it's very intoxicating."

Her mouth opens slightly as the words fall out of my mouth. Those beautiful light orange eyes are staring at me in wonder. I'm tired of chasing her. I will not leave, as she requests.

"I have to think about her. She's your mother, but she has the power to do harm to me and my mother, and to be honest, she's my enemy. We could never be anything."

"Listen," I say, moving closer to her. "I'm not leaving this porch, I'm coming inside, and you are safe with me." Her heart starts beating faster. Reseda is looking around like she doesn't know whether to run or surrender.

"Prince-"

"Layern."

"Layern, you are one stubborn dragon." She gives me a wicked smile. "Yet, you are still not coming in. Now take your hand off me. I'm tired."

"I'm tired too, and I could help you relax. I can make you feel better than you have ever felt."

"NO."

"Oh, yes," I say. I move quickly, placing my hands on her shoulders, running my hands slowly down her arms, keeping eye contact with her. I keep my legs steady, she makes me weak just being around her. My hands move slowly to her breasts. "Ahh," she moans. I gently circle her nipples with my thumbs through her thin blue dress, feeling the heat exit her body, making my sex even harder. My hands leave her breasts as I slowly move my body down hers, placing my, now extremely hot, hands on her thighs, squeezing gently.

"You like that?" I ask, rubbing my head in the center of her pelvic area.

35

"Layern, my neighbors are probably looking."

"Let me inside, then." She pauses for only a second before twisting the knob and pushing the door open. I glance down at her black four-inch heels. "Nice shoes," I say.

"Layern, just come in, I don't want to talk about my shoes," she says, breathless.

"I could make you scream out in pleasure right here, besides, I like those heels." I look up, meeting her eyes, and the flicker of her eyes shows her beast is aroused too.

"Please, Layern, come inside, I want you to come inside," she pleads.

Making her suffer more, I begin softly biting her inner thighs, becoming more aroused myself by the second. I bite her a couple more times before standing.

"Why are you concerned about your neighbors? They're just humans."

"Yeah, well, some of them are not all human," she says, turning to walk into her house. I stand on her porch looking around, noticing I don't hear anything, it's too quiet. "Are you coming?"

"Yes," I say, walking inside, "I'm coming, but I'll make sure you come too."

"I do hope so."

I walk slowly over to her, pulling my shirt over my head. Her eyes widen and a smile appears. She starts to unbutton her dress, exposing a red lace bra.

"Don't hold back, scream, bite. Do whatever you have to, but I can't guarantee gentle the first time. Maybe the second or third time tonight."

"I'm no virgin," she says, smiling, "and if you need to scream, don't be shy."

I push her up against the wall, dropping to my knees. My body aches for a taste of her honey. Sliding my hands up her legs, finding her sex, I pull gently on her light red pubic hair. Her hand pushes my head forward, she wants it bad. I knew she would. I grin as I begin sliding her dress around her waist, she is now exposed to me. "You smell delicious, let's see if you taste the same." I don't give her a chance to reply. My hands open her folds and I'm greeted with a swollen nub and her glistening honey. I take one slow, deliberate lick and feel her legs tremble. I want to say the same thing, because after that taste, I need more a lot more. I don't hesitate, and push my tongue inside her comfort zone, sliding it in and out. I hear her moans and they are getting louder and I know she's close, damn I'm close, but I have better control, so I place my mouth over her clitoris and suck hard, slipping in two fingers, twisting and turning. Reseda's hands are in my hair and she is pulling hard. I can feel that she's about to burst and then she does, with a squeal I've never heard before. Then it dawns on me, it is her beast too. I smile, as it's always a pleasure to make the female beast have pleasure too. I stand, holding her as she slumps into my arms.

"Layern," she pants. "I think, I'm having another aftershock, I, oh, oh, ohhhhhh!" Reseda is gorgeous as she reaches her climax, and I want more.

"I need you now, the bedroom I don't need. Do you?

"No."

"Good," I say, pulling her dress over her head, "enough talking." Allowing one of my claws to come forth, I rip off her bra. It doesn't take me long to get completely naked, because clothes are something I don't wear a lot of. I stand back, admiring her body. It is like looking at a goddess. She is one of the most beautiful women I have ever seen. Reseda looks down as if she's ashamed. I will address this later. Right now, I need her. In a flash I'm pressing her up against the wall. Our lips meet and never part as my hands explore her body. The heat leaving my body is almost painful. She wraps her legs around my waist and I'm right at her entrance, which I have named the 'comfort zone.'

She's so tight, I know she's not a virgin, but I'm sure she has not had sex in a while. I push in slowly and we both moan, I think Reseda is moaning from a slight dash of pain, but my body feels like this is home. I lean my head forward, pressing soft kisses on her shoulder. One of my hands finds the back of her neck and the other grips her thigh, as I start a pace that we both can enjoy. Her body is gripping my sex and it's about to send me over the edge too early. A growl comes out of my mouth and she responds, growling back. I should be paying attention to her breast and the rest of her body, but I have to get my first climax. My pace picks up and she meets me with each thrust, moaning and growling at the same time. When I can no longer hold back, my hand leaves her neck and slams against the wall, causing permanent damage, to the wall.

We both slide down to the floor, still connected. I'm sure I have tired her out, but the selfishness in me is just getting started.

"Did I hurt you?" I ask. I become more aware that she's half human, and I'm pretty sure she's never been with a dragon before, I would have smelled the scent.

"Yes," Her voice is not much louder than a whisper, "but I'm better than fine, but now I have to face the reality, I should not have had sex… fabulous sex, with you. I have caused me and my mother a death sentence."

I frown at her words. I remove myself from her body. I stand and she tries to stand too. I smile as she realizes her legs are sore. I bend and pick her up, and place us both instantly in her bedroom, using the vanishing, or merr, gift that some dragons have. I lay her on her king-size bed.

"Ok, first, no one knows I'm here except Gemi. Secondly, my mother is not going to harm you."

She's lying on her back, and my hands roam her body. I will get a chance to touch every part of her beautiful body. Her nipples harden, and I notice their beautiful shade of pink. I lean down and wrap my mouth around one, pulling softly and placing a kiss right on the tip. Her body arches upward.

"Mmm, ahhh, Layern, please, I can't have a serious conversation with you when you do that."

"Do what? This?" I ask, cupping her breast. I take the other breast into my mouth and give a little bite, and then place another soft kiss at the head of that lovely nipple.

"Oh, yes… please, I can't think with your mouth doing that," she begs. She doesn't really want me to stop. She makes no move to push me away. I go a little further and slide my hand down her abdomen, reaching her comfort zone and spreading her folds. Her legs slide further apart. Is she is just as naughty as I am? I will find out. My eyes meet hers, and I want more. Her breathing is rasped and fast, her chest falls and rises. I can't stop watching her, my fingers get to know her comfort zone more, rubbing her harder. Her mouth opens with just one word: 'YES!' I lick my lips, knowing it will be a long night. I slip in one finger, then another, until I have three fingers inside her. She moans, and I watch as her body unfolds before me. I close my eyes as she tightens around my fingers. I pull them out quickly, as I want to be inside her as she climaxes. Her whimper is sexy as her need is consuming. My body covers hers and I hold my weight with my arms rested beside her head. Something stunning happens as I slide into her and start the movements of the best dance ever. She arches her back, and my head falls back and we reach ecstasy together. We are both panting now.

"I can't think around you," she says.

"The feeling is mutual. I like you. I see you like me too, so how about we worry about everything else later, but just for tonight, can we just enjoy each other without mentioning my mother, please," I beg. She stares at me, thinking of my words. I don't want to think about anything but her. My mother's name does not need to be brought up at all. I wait for her answer.

"Ok, if you promise to give me a choice to end this to save my mother's life."

"I will promise to talk with you about this problem," I say, "but letting you go, no, I will not promise you that."

"You are one stubborn dragon," she says, smiling. I smile back at her.

"Stay in bed, I'm going to get us some things we will need, I plan on keeping you in this bed." I slide out of her.

"What if I want to take a shower?"

I turn and look at her strangely, she must not understand.

"No showers until we are done, I like the smell of me on you and you on me." I walk out of her room. I hear my cell phone ringing as I step into the kitchen. Damn, Hawken! I run and get the phone.

"What?"

"You need to get home soon," Hawken snaps, "Our mother is asking about you. Where is Gemi? I've been calling him too, he's not answering his phone." This brother right here has no loyalty to his brothers, except to come with some bad news. I try to remember his curse, but it's hard when you just want to set his lips on fire when he speaks.

"I'll be home tomorrow, and Gemi can handle himself, he is more than likely having a good time. Like I am."

"Well, I won't cover for you, so get your asses back home, brother."

"Brother, we will be home tomorrow. You worry about your secret, I know."

The cell phone goes dead. I walk back into the kitchen and open the fridge. I need energy food for her. I find some Greek yogurt, almonds, some Hershey's dark chocolate and some raw spinach. This should work. I pack my arms with all of these, and make sure to stuff water bottles under my arms. I climb the stairs three at a time, quickly reaching the top. I walk into the room and find her sleeping, not on my watch, Reseda, when I say all night, all night is what I mean.

RESEDA

I fall asleep not long after Layern walks out of the room. I have had so many orgasms back to back. I didn't know it was even possible. I promised him the night, but I'm so sleepy. I find myself in a beautiful dream, walking on the beach, the water is so blue, like Layern's eyes. I smile and see a very large blue dragon coming towards me. It's beautiful, with wings and huge, strong legs. His arms are connected to the wings by a thin membrane. He lands right in front of me. I take a step back without thinking. I have seen dragons before, but never a Draglen brother up close. They are much bigger than other dragons, and I can say for myself, yes, they are huge. The dragon blows from its mouth, and blue smoke comes out and surrounds me, I enjoy the feeling of it. I feel arms come around my waist, and know Layern is with me now. I have heard of them being able to enter your dreams. Not all dragons have this gift, but the rumor is that all the Draglen brothers can do this.

"You trying to sleep on me, sexy?"

"Who, me? Why would I need rest after all those orgasms?"

"My beast likes you, Reseda, my beautiful Lecena," he says. I know that means flower. I can't fall for Layern. It's wrong, besides all the obvious reasons. I take a deep breath, enjoying his touch. We stand in silence for a few seconds, as the dream comes to an end and I see Layern sitting next to me with food in his arms. I smile, because he looks truly happy, wow!

"Was the dream real?" I ask.

"What do you think?"

I shake my head, focusing my attention on the various foods. He begins to set the food on my nightstand. I take this time to enjoy his amazing body. He's gorgeous. I can't believe those hands and lips were on me."What are you thinking?" he asks. He places his hands on my thighs and begins a very gentle massage. My body is going weak with just this contact. "I'm thinking why did you bring tons of food up here, and nothing matches, Pri...Layern."

"I'm glad you caught yourself, it's Layern, ok?

"Ok."

"Now, the food is fuel, for you," he says, picking up some Greek yogurt and scooping up a huge amount in a tablespoon. "I plan on having you up all night, but I have to feed your human side to keep you awake." He brings the spoon to my mouth very slowly, not breaking eye contact. Why is this so hot to me?

"Open," he says. I just do it, and my mouth is filled with

delicious vanilla Greek yogurt.

"Mmm…very good!" I say, enjoying the taste. He picks up a few pieces of spinach and starts feeding them to me, one by one. He keeps one hand on my thigh, and through the sheet he pushes his hand farther up my leg until he brushes against my sex. I'm going to explode, with him feeding me and playing with my body through the sheet.

"Baby, I just want you to enjoy, eat." I'm greeted with dark chocolate, and my eyes roll back. I love dark chocolate. It's so good. "I think you are energized for another round now," he says.

My body bows to him. I want him so badly, and it doesn't take long before he is leaning over me, licking my lips, waiting for me to open. I do without hesitation. I want this. In fact, I need this. The sheet is removed and Layern moves between my legs, hovering over me, but maintaining the deep kiss. Our tongues are one and I'm melting like ice cream. Layern's mouth feels like ecstasy. The head of his sex is right at my entrance, but he waits. He sucks my breasts, like he can't stop. I need him inside me.

"Layern, please," I beg. He laughs and gently slides inside me, and it feels right. I have never felt this good during sex.

"Baby, you feel so good, it's my private comfort zone," he whispers in my ear. Our bodies have a rhythm that is slow, but intense. His beast growls, and I fall deep into a bliss of pleasure.

***

Daylight comes and he finally allows me to sleep, but now I don't want to go. We end up talking. I can't express enough how much I hate Queen Nala, she's his mother, but I hate her. We talk of my mother's life, my life, how it has been in constant turmoil. How we are always wondering if she will make good on her promise.

"Seda, why are you so quiet?" Layern asks, "I want to know more about you." My head is on his chest and I'm taking in how wonderful he smells. His hands are in my hair, and it feels so good to have the comfort of a man. I sigh, knowing I can't tell him how I really feel. This is only for today, but he has to go back home, and I have to stay here and run my shop downtown. Wait, did he call me Seda? Wow! "Umm...did you call me Seda?" I ask, smiling.

"Yes, I did. Is that a problem?"

"No, I just never had anyone call me by a nickname before, it's weird."

"Well, I will have more nicknames for you, especially your comfort zone." He laughs. I turn and face him, and I'm taken aback by those blue eyes. I can't help but reach out, touching his face softly. His eyes close and he looks relaxed. I take this time to rub my hands through his short, soft, brown hair. I can't believe I'm lying next to him, naked. I shake my head in disbelief.

"Mmm, Seda, keep touching me with those soft hands and I will have you again." My hands explore his hair, chest, lips, even his arms. I turn to lie back down, feeling a little overwhelmed. This feeling with him is blissful, but I know this cannot work, not ever.

"Layern, you are amazing. You have given me a night that I

will remember forever, but I-"

"Don't, I told you if I want to pursue this, us, I can and I will. Stop worrying so much. I will take care of everything. Ok?"

"No, it's not ok, Layern." I say harshly. "I can't risk my mother's life to have fabulous sex with you. And I will remind you that your mother, Queen Nala, has not given me an option. I could be killed on sight if she knew I sneaked into Kalin. I like sex with you, but not enough to betray my mother." He is quiet for only a few seconds before I'm flipped on my back and he has both my hands gripped in one of his.

"Seda, I love the speech you just made. It was… entertaining." He pauses to take a deep breath. His eyes close for a second, and as he opens them the blue is a mixture of shades of blue, almost mesmertizing. "I can get fabulous sex any time I want, with anyone I want. I'm asking you to trust, for once in your life, and know that I will not hurt you, and I will make you a promise that neither you nor your mother will be harmed." He growls. His thighs push my legs far apart, and he's inside me, thrusting hard and fast. I don't have time to think. He bends and takes my breast into his mouth, sucking my nipple. My hands are released and I feel him grab my thighs. He sets a punishing, thrusting pace. I try to keep up, but I can't.

"Lay… Lay… oh, my," I moan.

"Seda, beautiful, I think I'll keep you." Those words are my release and I scream out in pleasure: 'ahhhhhh!' He follows me with his own release, speeding his pace. I finally open my eyes to a smiling Layern. I think I want him too.

"I think a bath will do me good, right now." I smile. Layern has a way of making me forget my worries, only for a second.

"I'll go run the water, we both can get in."

"Oh, ok." I say. Layern removes himself from me and drops a sweet kiss on my forehead. It seems so sexy, yet it was just a kiss on my forehead, and I could have asked for more. I watch him walk into my bathroom, and boy, does he have a sexy-ass walk. I hear the water come on, and then I smell something. Delicious, but different, not food. He comes strolling back in with such authority. He doesn't listen at all. He's such a stubborn dragon.

"You ready, Seda?"

I smile. He says that so sweetly. It's easy to fall for Layern Draglen. I guess the rumors are true. He's a weakness for females of all kinds.

"Yes, I'm ready," I say breathlessly. He takes my breath away. He bends, scoops me up and walks into the bathroom, where a tub is almost full of beautiful blue water. The smell in the bathroom is amazing. I've never smelled anything like it.

He steps into the tub with me still in his arms, lowering us both into the water, which spills over onto the floor.

"Layern, my floor is all wet now." I frown. He laughs and blows over the floor with his breath, and it's instantly dry.

"The pleasure of being a dragon," he grins. "I want to ask you something. I'm sure you know I have a gift, right?"

Shit yes, I know. Did he pick up that I hate his mother, oh

God, I hope he didn't pick that up.

"Umm, yes, why do you ask?"

"I'm having trouble picking up your thoughts. Why are you guarded so well?" he asks. I lean back on his chest, and he starts a slow, but gratifying, massage of my breasts. I moan without thinking: "Mmmmm." He continues sliding his hand down, pushing my legs farther apart, and then slipping two fingers into my sex. He has asked me a question, and I'm not sure if I can speak with his hands all over me.

"Seda..." Layern cracks up laughing. "Lecena, did you hear my question?"

"Yes, I heard you, it's very distracting to think when your hands are, ahhh... magic!" I stumble the words out.

"Well, should I stop?"

"NO!"

"Shhh, calm, my beautiful flower. I don't plan on it, forget the question for now. I need to give you more pleasure."

"Can I show you something?"

"Yes."

I take a deep breath and blow out, and fire comes out, making a beautiful blaze on top of the water. The mixture of the blue and red fire looks amazing. I've never been able to try it with anyone before. I hope he likes it. I feel his hand go out, placing his fingers in the flames. I turn and see him smile.

"Seda, that's amazing, thank you for sharing it with me."

"You're welcome." I feel shy all of a sudden. Why should I be so open with Layern? It's not long before I turn around in the tub and straddle his hips. Layern is ready, and I position him and slide him in inch by inch. I finally adjust to this position and our moans are loud as I begin a rhythm with him.

***

We are both very hungry after a night of sex. I think some would label it as passion, but I know this is Prince Layern, and the rumor is that he has loved only once and has never loved again. I don't mind. It was the best sex I will probably ever have. He sits at my table as I prepare us both breakfast. I decide to cook bacon, along with sausage, eggs, toast, hash browns, and some fruit as well. I hope it's enough. Dragons can eat, I know for sure. I've seen it first hand. I'm only half dragon, and I can out-eat any human man. I'm cooking when I hear the doorbell.

"Shit!" Layern growls.

"What? It's more than likely Palmer. I'll get rid of him."

"It's Gemi, my brother, I'll let him in." Layern says. He comes back in with Gemi. I didn't get a good look at him last night dancing, but he's standing in my kitchen in the light, and damn. He has the most amazing body, with the sexiest gray eyes I've ever seen. I stop cooking and start staring.

"Seda, please don't have me fight my brother." Layern raises a brow at me. I feel embarrassed now, so I turn and finish the hash browns.

"We have to go," I hear Gemi tell Layern.

"I know, I'm going to eat breakfast, I would offer you some, but I sense you are eager to leave."

"Yes, Mother is searching for us."

"I know, Hawken called. Brother, we will leave. Please have a seat. Reseda is cooking." There was silence as if they were speaking to each other in their heads. I know the Draglen Brothers have that ability. I speak to break the building tension.

"Do you mind if I put on some music?" I ask. Both brothers look at me, and I turn quickly, feeling a lustful desire for Layern again. I mean, Gemi is handsome, but I just did some amazing things with Layern, and he's the notorious Prince Layern.

"Seda, yes, music would be great," Layern says. He and Gemi go back to the table and snack on the fruit I have placed out. I can't believe I'm feeding royalty. I go over to my stereo system and put on Erykah Badu. I dance back to the stove. I'm immersed in my cooking when I feel arms around me.

"Thank you."

"You don't have to thank me." I say. I know he will be leaving soon, which is best. I just wish I didn't have a ban on me. I could have another night with him.

"Wow, I felt that, Lecena, you will have many nights with me."

I gasp, not sure what to say. I finish cooking breakfast, and we all begin to eat in silence. I become sad as Layern and Gemi stand. I know he is leaving and it's only been one night, but I feel so comfortable with him. Gemi thanks me for the food, and waits out in the foyer.

"I'll be back," Layern says, smiling. He leans in, giving me a deep, intense kiss. I find my hand going around his neck, pulling him as close as possible.

"I understand, Layern…"

"Shhh… see you soon, Lecena," he says. He turns and leaves before I can speak. I sit on the floor in the foyer, wondering how I fell for one of Queen Nala's sons. It might be time for me to move.

LAYERN

We arrive in my section of the castle. Gemi and I nod to each other and head to our rooms. On my walk to my room, I'm stopped by a servant.

"Prince Layern, please forgive me for this interruption, but Queen Nala, mother of the Draglen brothers, requests your presence, now." She speaks with her head bowed.

"Thank you, you may leave now."

Fuck, I don't want to deal with Queen Nala. I turn around and make my way to her favorite place, the gardens. She is sitting on one of the benches, feeding the birds.

"Ah, my son. Why do you have to be so stubborn?" she asks. I say nothing. It's a trap. "I'm not trying to trap you, Prince, I simply would like to know, how is the woman you lay with last night?"

"Queen Nala, Mother of Draglen descendants, I ask humbly to speak freely," I say.

"I wouldn't have it any other way, my son."

"First, why are you watching whom I lie with?"

"I'm not watching, I usually never care, but from you I sensed a feeling deeper than just a good lay, my son. I became curious, and looked further into this woman."

"Who is she to you?"

"Someone you need to stay clear of, I'll handle her."

"You will not handle her, I would like to see her again," I say. My feelings are hidden right now.

"Ah, you are getting good at your gift, I will make you an offer. You may see her, if you understand she cannot be anything but pleasure to you."

"Ok."

"I'm not finished, you must end this before your brother's first Young is born, understand?"

Shiiiiiit!!! Why does everything have to be on her terms? I can't believe her. I stare disbelievingly at her for a few minutes.

"Fine," I say, turning to walk away.

"Son, I love you very much, but make no mistake- this is something you don't want to challenge me on. That thing you are lying with should not be living, so if you cross me I will personally take a trip to her home in Louisiana and rip her head off with a smile."

We glare at each other before I speak.

"I would expect nothing less from you, Mother."

"Great! Now go see if your brother needs help with the

celebration. We are preparing for the first Young among my Youngs. How exciting!" She beams. What did my father see in her?

I turn and leave the gardens. I need some time to think, so I head to my room. If I do what she wants, I'm using Reseda, but if I don't, my mother could still pay her a visit and kill her. I make it to my room, and stand on my terrace looking at our land. It's beautiful, just like Reseda. I have to see her, to protect her, but keeping my feelings out is going to be impossible. I've never felt so good with a woman before, and she ignites something in me. I never thought a woman could do that for me again, but Reseda is so delicate, but strong. I want more of her. I turn, feeling my brother close, Showken of course. I smile.

"Come in, brother, it's unlocked."

"There's my brother who finds his nasty again when I find my Wella!" Showken smiles.

"Let's not talk about me, how is my beautiful sister doing, ready for the big celebration?"

"Well, she knows a party is going to happen, I didn't tell her everyone in Cortamagen will be there."

I burst into laughter.

"She's going to kill you. Tell her."

"Do you remember how Marilyn could be difficult before I made her my Wella?"

"Yes."

"Well, she's scary now. She sometimes breathes fire. I know

it's because she carries my Young, the problem is the fire hurts."

We both crack up laughing now.

"Now that we are laughing, our mother is upset about something, and Draken says you're lying with an enemy of hers. Is that true?"

"The truth is our mother is crazy, and wants to kill one of our kind. Reseda is half dragon, why is Queen Nala so against her?"

"Reseda, very different name. Listen, I'm backing you no matter what, but I never thought our mother could want to pay a visit to Earth, but apparently she's willing to, according to Draken."

"Yes, she's been real clear about me seeing Reseda, I would just like to know the real story."

"Well, try not to worry about it tonight, it's a huge party and it's in my and my Wella's honor. Plus, plenty of dragon women to pick from."

Showken gives me a huge smile and I just shake my head. He leaves, after some encouragement. I push my hand into my pocket, pulling out Reseda's ripped panties. Her scent is still on them, making me smile. I can't wait to see her, but I have to be here for my brother and his Wella. Soon a Young will be in the castle. I decide to go for a quick flight before preparing for tonight. Flying is therapeutic, and besides, my beast would like to get out.

***

The celebration is starting soon. Well, I'm pretty sure it will be late. Showken can't keep his hands off his Wella. I'm in my ocean blue pants, they're loose for dancing. We are all on the evno. My brothers are lined up standing, except for Draken and Cess. They are seated with my father and mother. The drums and horns begin to blow as Showken and Marilyn walk out. Her expression is pure shock. Everyone wants to see Marilyn. She is showing now. The ceremony has started with my father giving a speech. I begin to tune out everyone as my mind drifts back to Reseda. She's beyond stunning, but she's also tough. I glance at Queen Nala, only to confirm my suspicions of her watching me. I come back mentally into the ceremony as it's my turn to give Marilyn a gift.

"Greetings, my sister. I'm very happy for you and my brother. The Young you carry will be one of many, if I know my brother. Take this gift for my brocur or siscur." It's customary to hand the gift to my brother. So I hand him a blue box, decorated with jewels. Showken opens the box to find three filled blue crystal bottles. He smiles. Bruiser, our new castle pet, barks at me, then comes to give me a gentle nudge. I rub his head, smiling. Showken accepted him, now he has grown on all of us.

"He or she will need these three wishes with you as a father," I say. Showken and I hug, and share a good laugh.

I hear Warton behind me. "That's a weak gift." I turn, glaring at my warrior brother. He can be a menace.

"Thanks, Layern," Showken replies. I move along to let my other brothers give their gifts. Beauka has given them a tea set for the Young, saying that she will teach the Young how to make special teas. Marilyn thinks this is exciting news. My brothers and I just look at her. She's one strange dragon.

It doesn't take long before we are eating, dancing and having a good time. There were many gifts for Showken and Marilyn at the steps of the evno. I dance with a few dragon shifters, but my mind is on Reseda and what she is doing. Her little human friend Palmer really wants her, and I can't stay away too long. She might decide to be with him.

I take a seat to watch the party, and how Cess and Beauka cannot keep their hands off Marilyn's belly. I even see Brumen and Fewton rub her belly. Domlen is keeping his distance after his gift, and so is Hawken. I look for Gemi and find him eating, but I feel as though his mind is sad. He truly wants a Wella.

"Brother, you enjoying yourself?" Draken comes and sits with me. He is smiling. It's amazing what Cess has done. He may turn out to be an alright King someday.

"Yes, I'm very happy for our brother and his Wella."

"But..."

"It's so amazing," I say, "how you changed after you took Cess as your Wella."

"I'm trying to be a fucking caring brother, Layern, because I know the order mother gave you, but don't confuse yourself. I really don't give a fuck."

"That's the Draken I know."

"Fuck you."

"No, but thanks, brother."

"Right, going to check on my Wella." He stands.

"Thanks."

"Any time."

Draken leaves and I'm still sitting and thinking about Reseda. I'm going to have to use Reseda in order to see her, reporting back to Queen Nala. I need to find out what has gotten my mother so upset about a regular dragon. I watch as she and King Dramen dance. The entire country is watching and cheering as the King and Queen of Cortamagen dance for Showken and Marilyn. It's very prestigious to have the King dance for you. This Young will be the light of the castle.

It's not long before the party really starts and everyone is dancing, including me. I find a very lovely dragon shifter who wants to lie with me. I don't bother to ask her name. Her arousal is heavy in the air. My brothers are encouraging me to take her to bed. They are just happy I'm over Maka. I can say I'm very pleased about that as well. If it were any other time, I would have had this female dragon already, but Reseda has happened. I can't help but wonder if I'm in her thoughts too. I know her friend Palmer is around, trying to undo all I've done, but it won't work. I feel sorry for him. He's carrying a torch for someone who will never be able to love him. The female I'm dancing with speaks, breaking into my thoughts.

"Prince Layern," she says seductively, "I'm willing to please you in any way you want."

"What is your name?" I ask.

"My name is Hilta, Prince Layern."

I sniff around her neck and really start dancing with her. I want to know her motives, as I have a feeling sex is not the only thing she's willing to do.

"Ah, I see now, you think I want a Giver?"

"Oh, Prince Layern, if you would have me I would be so grateful."

I search her eyes, only to see she's serious. She just wants to please me.

"I would never take you as my Wella."

"I understand, Prince Layern, it would still be a great honor to pleasure you, and I'm ready to start tonight if you will have me."

We dance in silence. Every female dragon would love to be a Giver to a Draglen brother. I seek her thoughts, she just wants to please me. As I look her up and down, guilt covers me. I'm not committed to anyone, yet a pull towards Reseda can't be ignored. Hilta has such hope in her eyes. I'll test her out and see if I like her.

"I'll try you for one night, Hilta, but not tonight. I have some things to do."

"Yes Prince Layern, I will be ready."

"I'm sure you will, Hilta." I smile. She in return gives me a very pleasing smile. I could find time to see if she will be a good Giver for the future. I'm not searching for a Giver, I can have sex with whomever I want, including her. The song changes and I dismiss Hilta. I'm really missing Seda, smiling to myself at the nickname.

I leave the celebration after making my rounds to say goodbye to my brother and his Wella, and to Cess, although my insane future King has a rule about touching Cess, even a friendly touch. I simply give her a smile, and a nod goodbye. Finally making it to my own private waters. I decide on a late swim. As I'm undressing, I feel eyes on me. I turn and see Hilta.

"You don't understand 'consider'?" I ask, feeling a little annoyed.

"Oh, Prince Layern, I just thought maybe if we were alone you could get a feel of how eager I am to pleasure you."

I watch as she slides out of her dress, standing naked before me. She's beautiful, with long black hair, grey eyes, full lips and perfect breasts. All that and I can't even get hard with her standing before me.

"Put your dress back on, and go."

"I- I'm sorry. Please give me another chance."

"Listen, please stop begging, that is my brother's thing. I'm sorry, I'm not looking for a Giver."

Her head hangs low and the tears start right away. I can't believe this shit.

"Why are you crying?"

She doesn't answer, only shakes her head. I cock my head to the side trying to get a read on her. She's hiding something. Narrowing my eyes, I turn up my gift, only to get flashes, but enough to anger me.

"You work for Queen Nala?" I ask. I'm towering over her. I'm so angry I could breathe fire. She falls down on her knees, asking for forgiveness.

"Sio, sio, sio," she repeats over and over.

I turn to leave, but not before I dish out a punishment for her.

"You tried to deceive a Draglen brother, yes, my mother the Queen is powerful, but you must remember I carry the blood, and for that, this is your punishment. If I lay eyes on you again, I will rip you from limb to limb. Now go!" I yell, walking away quickly before I rip her head off.

I pace the hall of the castle, angered for numerous reasons, but it would be disrespectful to leave now. I have to wait three days. FUCK!!! I'm usually an easy- going guy, but this trick my mother has just pulled brings out the beast. I hear Gemi, Fewton and Brumen walking up.

"We're heading to Noke for some female pleasure. Do you want to join us?" Fewton asks me.

I look at my brothers and they instantly know I'm upset. My eyes are all beast, and I could transform right in this castle and rip it apart.

"Layern, what's got you upset?" Fewton asks. I'm having difficulty speaking, Queen Nala is overstepping herself. I pace a little more without speaking, then I stop and yell:

"OUR FUCKING MOTHER IS EVIL!" and start pacing again.

"What did she do, brother?" Gemi asks, sternly. He knows all too well how our mother can be.

"Queen Nala, our mother, had the female dragon come earlier, and offer herself as a Giver, for the sole purpose of deterring me from Reseda," I growl.

"Who is Reseda?" Brumen asks. His voice is so deep it sends a tremble through us when he talks. He is the brother that is quiet, but truly is the beast among the brothers.

"She's this very sexy half-dragon that our mother hates, and the poor female is banned from Kalin."

"How did you meet her, then?"

"She sneaks into Noke, and I had a dance with her." I shrug. That was an amazing dance. She has the perfect afla.

My brothers look at me, as I close my eyes remembering our dance, and a very long night. Yes, I need more.

"What are you going to do? We all know the stipulation that's on you if you continue to see her," Gemi says.

"Oh I'm going to see her," I snap, "come hell or high water."

"Ok, that's cool with me," Fewton says, smiling, "but for three days you are stuck, so let's go and have some fun in Noke?" He's ready, he loves to flirt and just be around women all the time. He's recently recovering from the burn Draken dished out for rubbing Cess' hair. I smile, remembering that day. I think for a minute and I do need to release stress, I don't want to go without sex for more than twenty-four hours. I have to make up for five years.

"I'm with you, brothers," I say. "Let's head to Noke for fun."

My brothers and I don't waste any time getting to the gardens and transforming into full dragons. I plan on pushing Reseda out of my head for three days, but the minute I can leave, I'm going back to her. I need to know more about her, and why my mother hates her. I might find her mother and see if can get some information. Whatever my mother is afraid of, I will make sure to expose the secret. I don't like tricks, not even from Queen Nala. I hear a growl coming from Brumen, my wing has touched him and caused him to stumble in mid-air. Soon we land in Noke. Fun, sex and even more sex.

RESEDA

It's been three days. I haven't heard anything from Layern. He just fucked me and disappeared. I've been losing my mind over how I just let him use me. Palmer comes over every morning, to check on me, and I don't have the energy to let him in the door. I can't believe it, I thought he could feel something for me. I should have known, he's her son. I've been so upset. He did give me the best sex I've ever experienced, and I guess I should be grateful, but I was hoping he might want to see me again. I'm done with him. I don't care to see him ever again. I should never have let him lie down with me. My father would be so disappointed. He protected me. I feel so lost without my dad. He was the best, but now he's gone. I pull myself out of bed, and decide a hot bath is what I need. I'm still sore from Layern. I decide to change my sheets today, too. The smell of him on my bed only makes me angry. I will go to my dad's grave and sit with him. It may sound silly to some, but it's my only connection to him. He would know how to make me feel better. Why did Queen Nala take my father from me? Three hundred years was not long enough, and now I'm stuck on Earth, where I don't fit in.

I strip the bedding, leaving it in the middle of the floor, slip out of my t-shirt and head straight for the bath. After making the water as hot as possible, I blow my breath to make it hotter. I need to feel the heat. After pouring in some oils, I slip into the water. The doorbell rings and I hear lots of banging.

"RESEDA, PLEASE ANSWER THE DOOR!" Palmer yells. I close my eyes and hope he leaves. "I'M NOT LEAVING!" How the hell did he know what I was thinking? I shake my head and continue to soak. Then I hear my door opening. I'm going to kill him.

"RESEDA, WHERE ARE YOU!"

"I'M IN THE TUB, ASSHOLE!"

I hear him at the bathroom door, breathing like a madman.

"I'm sorry, I picked the lock and came in, Reseda, I've not seen you out, your shop manager says you called off for a week. What happened, please talk to me? I'm your friend." I hear such pain in his voice. I hate to shut him out, but I can't tell him the truth. Besides, he only wants into my bed too.

"Go away, please," I say.

"NO!"

"I'm trying to be real nice," I say, "but Palmer, you don't want to see my ugly side, ever. It's like a fire that spreads."

"I don't care how you threaten me, I'm not leaving until I see your face."

Fine, he wants to see something. I climb out of the tub and yank the door open, completely naked. I know that's what he wants.

"Oh damn, Reseda, why are you naked, but damn!" He's so turned on by my just standing in front of him dripping wet and very angry.

"Now, you see me, and all that you have been waiting to see, can you go now and leave me the fuck alone. When I need to talk, that's when I will call, got it?" I raise my brows. He is so distracted I just slam the door in his face. Fucking men, doesn't matter if they are a dragon or human, pussy always distracts them.

"Reseda, I'm sorry, but you came out here naked on purpose. Does this have anything to do with that guy you were dancing with?"

"GET THE FUCK OUT OF MY HOUSE!" I yell. I don't want to think about him.

"Reseda, please," he begs. I sigh, and tears flow down my face. How can I treat my only friend like this? This is for his benefit. I'm different, and should have never befriended him. I am going to be alone. This is the hand I've been dealt. After he pleads for another ten minutes, I hear him leave. I sink into the tub and have myself a good cry.

***

Later that day, I dress and head to the cemetery where my father is buried. I go there when I need to be near him. I find his name quickly. John Nolan Fire. What a name, right? I sit in front of his tombstone, laying my hands over his name. I find myself sobbing, with my hand on my dad's name. I can't believe it's been ten years. I pull myself together and begin a one- ided conversation.

"Hi, Dad, I know it's been three months since I came to see you. I'm sorry. I miss you so much. You would not be pleased with me right now, Dad. I've been so stupid." I take a couple of deep breaths. I reach into my purse and pull out a bottle of wine and a glass. I always drink a glass of wine at my father's grave. It was our tradition to talk over wine.

"You know my friend Palmer, or he might not want to be my friend any more. I just behaved like an asshole to him, and he only wanted to know if I was alright. I disobeyed you, Dad. I have been sneaking into Noke to see Mom, and I ran into a Draglen brother." More tears roll down my face. My dad always told me to stay away. He told me, that once he was gone, I must stay away from Noke. I just missed my mother so much. Now, I might have given her a death sentence.

"Dad, I know everything you have taught me, but Layern, I mean Prince Layern, was so persistent. Now I feel like a piece of meat. I thought I could sleep with him and not feel anything, but it didn't work. He left three days ago, and I've not heard one word from him." My anger is building now, so I fill my glass again and toss it back.

"I know if you were here you would say stay away from him, and believe me, Dad, I will. I'm never going to see him again. He got what he wanted, and I guess I did too. Yes, Dad, I said that, I wanted sex from him, just never thought I wanted more. Now I know that will never happen. I have to figure out how to apologize to Palmer. He's such a good friend. You would have liked him, Dad. He's funny, kind, and handsome, but I feel nothing for him beyond friendship. I'm always going to be alone. Well, here's to life being a bitch!" I pour take the rest of the wine and drink it down. I kiss my dad's tombstone, and leave the bottle of wine with the glass, next to his grave.

I go on a mission to find Palmer. It's late in the evening now, and he might be having a drink at our favorite bar. I spot him instantly. He's drinking Jack Daniels, he's really hurt or really pissed. Ok, Reseda, swallow your pride and say you're sorry. I walk over and take a seat next to him. He looks up at me, and he looks so sad.

"I'll take two of what he's having," I say to Kimmy the bartender. He nods.

You here to hurt me some more?" Palmer asks. I wince, remembering how mean I've been. My dad would be so ashamed. He tried to make sure I was a kind person, always. He knew that my beast could get angry and violent.

"No, I'm here to beg for forgiveness," I say, "I'm so sorry. I didn't mean to speak to you like that. I was angry." My drinks are placed in front of me. I slide one over to Palmer, and we both take a long sip.

"Who upset you?"

"Let's just forget about it," I say. "I'm over it, and would like to spend the day with my friend, begging for forgiveness." I look at him in the mirror in front of us. I hope he can forgive me. Our eyes meet. He gives me a smile and I know I'm forgiven.

"Of course I forgive you. I could never stay mad at you, but I will take the begging today." He chuckles.

"Yes, I'm sure you will, but I will do it happily. I was not myself earlier."

"You can say that again," he says, finishing his glass, "I've never seen you that angry, in fact. Your eyes were really weird. I was a little scared." Shit, I don't ever want to hurt anyone because of anger. My beast must have tried to get out. I'm so glad he didn't get hurt. My beast is very wild.

"I'm sorry I scared you, I didn't mean to," I say. "Listen, how about we go get some food from the store and I cook a big meal, and we eat and watch movies all night?"

"That sounds like fun, and I get to pick the meal you cook?"

"Yes, I'm begging for forgiveness, remember?"

He says yes and we both laugh. We head to the store to pick up some fresh catfish, okra, and corn on the cob. Palmer has also requested my famous strawberry cheesecake, but I already have everything at my house for that. We make it to my house, and we laugh and talk as I cook. It almost takes away the pain of Layern, almost. He pops into my thoughts often. I push those thoughts way into the back of my mind.

Palmer and I eat and watch movies all night. It is just like old times. I am finally forgiven, and around four a.m. he falls asleep. I slept nearly three days, so I'm not tired. I finish off the rest of the food and clean the kitchen. After putting away the dessert, I place a pillow under Palmer's head, and I finally go up to my room where the pile of sheets is still on the floor. My mind says to just go get in the bed, but the lust says to lie on the sheets. Reasoning leaves me, and I curl into the sheets, smelling Layern's and my sex.

***

It's 7:00 am and I'm up before Palmer, even though I've only had a few hours of sleep. I go and give him a shake, only to hear him talk in his sleep.

"Willy Wonka candy is the best," he says. I try to contain my laugh, and nudge him again to wake up. "I like the caramel the best, though." I can't help myself - I'm bent over in hysterics.

"Huh, what?" Palmer says, stretching. I can't stop laughing, tears begin to pour down my face.

"You were talking in your sleep," I finally spit out. Palmer looks embarrassed, but I can't stop laughing. "Willy Wonka, huh?" I laugh even harder.

"Ha, very funny," Palmer says, standing.

"Oh, I needed that laugh, thanks a lot." I smile.

"Any time, at least you're not screaming at me to leave."

"No, I'm not screaming, but you need to go home. I plan on working from home, ordering new products for my candle shop."

"Oh ok, I need to go home. Your couch is not all that comfy."

I smile, knowing that my friendship with Palmer is safe. Things will get back to normal. I can move on. I walk Palmer out the door and watch him drive away. It's so peaceful outside. I take a deep breath and enter my house, walking back into the kitchen. Maybe I can get over Layern. I turn around to go upstairs, deciding to wash my sheets, but I bump right into a hard familiar chest. Shit.

"You forgot me?" Layern says, clenching his teeth. I try to push away, but my wrists are in his hands and they are being squeezed. I glare up at him. The nerve of him.

"Let me go, Prince Layern." I say. He doesn't speak. He just looks at me. Finally he releases my hands. I rub my wrists, trying to regain the circulation. I try to walk past him.

"Why did you let him stay the night with you? Let me be real clear," he snarls, "if I had even a vision he was in your bed, your friend would be dead." I don't care how angry Layern is, he decided not to speak to me for three days.

"No disrespect, Prince Layern, but fuck you!" I snap.

"Fuck me? No, I'm going to fuck you, Lecena." He smiles. My body goes a little weak when he says that. I'm going to hold my ground. My dad would say, 'Reseda, stand your ground, no matter how much you're tempted.' Of course, that was when I wanted to burn everything that pissed me off.

"I'm not going to lie with you, Prince Layern," I say calmly.

"Oh, such determination. I like that. Well, breakfast?"

"I'm not cooking you breakfast. I'm going to cook me breakfast."

"Be a good host, Seda, I'm still pissed you allowed that human to stay over with you. I came very close to taking him to Cortamagen and feeding him to some very hungry beasts I have."

Glaring at him, I see the truth in his eyes, and decide that for Palmer's safety, I should fix him breakfast.

"Fine, what might the prince want?"

"I'll have whatever you're cooking, Lecena."

"Can you please stop calling me that?"

"No."

My teeth grind as my temper rises. I cook breakfast and slide a plate over to him. We eat in silence and I get up to clear my plate. I'm looking out the window when hands come around my waist. Sucking in a deep breath, I try not to want his touch, but God, does he feel good against me.

"I'm sorry, I should have called, but my brother's Wella is with Young, and traditions kept me away from you. Forgive?"

Forgive? Why should I forgive him? He really doesn't need to ask for forgiveness. He is a prince and I'm nothing but a banned half-breed dragon who can't even see her mother openly. I feel him squeeze me tighter.

"Prince Layern, please."

"Layern, not Prince to you. I'm gone for three days, only because I had to support my brother, and you think I feel different?

73

You don't think much of me, Seda," he says. His lips touch the back of my neck and I feel a shiver go down my body. He sure knows how to make me react.

"I think-"

"I need you to listen to me. I like you, Reseda, I could have sex every hour with a different female if I chose. I don't want that, I want to spend time with you, break bread with you and have awesome, crazy, wild sex with you." His hands move from my waist until they are cupping my breasts. I close my eyes, enjoying his touch. I'm not sure how or when it happened, but my nightshirt is off, and all I'm wearing is a pair of shorts. It's like I'm outside my body watching this, and can't get myself to stop it. He pushes me onto the kitchen table, moaning in anticipation. I know it's going to be good. My self-consciousness is telling me to have some dignity, but my body is not listening. My back arches a little as he goes for my shorts.

"Oh Seda, a thong, I think I'll take this," he says. Bending down and using his mouth, he tears my shorts and thong apart. His lips find my sweet spot, and he begins a tender kiss. Closing my eyes, I try to will my body to stop, but I fail. My legs are pushed far apart as Layern dips his tongue inside me, causing a loud scream to leave me.

"Oh Lecena, you are like the sweetest pie I've ever had," he mumbles against my sex.

"Mmm, ahhh!" I can't even form words.

He spreads my folds apart and with one lick, I'm convulsing

on the table. He tongue- kisses my sex as my orgasm continues. It takes a minute for me to realize, he's now climbing onto the table with me, tapping my hip for me to turn over. This table is not going to hold. Layern throws my torn shorts on the floor, but my thong is not in sight. I don't have time to gain composure before he enters me from behind.

"I. DON"T. WANT. HIM. IN. THIS. HOUSE. AGAIN." He says each word with a slow thrust. What, I can't say anything. I'm losing it. He can't control me. The pace picks up, and the table is starting to move with each push. I'm getting closer to the counter and before I know it, my hands are gripping the edge. He slides out, leaving the tip in, making my body twitch. That's new, oh my, I can't take this pressure.

"PLEASE!!" I yell.

He gives me what I need, and after a few more thrusts, my body begins to shake as I explode. He soon follows. Our juices drip down our legs and onto the kitchen table. I can't believe this. My body doesn't last on my hands and knees, and I go limp and the table falls, and we just lie there panting. We stay in this position for a few minutes.

"Come on, Seda, I'll give you a bath, and then fix the table."

"Umm… I think we should just throw it out."

"No, I need to look at this table and remember the sweetest pie I've ever tasted was on this table, in your comfort zone." He smiles. I'm so tired, I can't even address his issue with Palmer. He carries me to my room and lays me down on the pile of sheets. I smile, because I know this is done on purpose. I hear the water, and the next thing I know, sleep has taken me.

***

I'm naked on top of the sheets on the floor, lying next to Layern. I can't believe this has happened again. He's truly a bad influence on me. I just promised myself that he would not have me, yet I'm naked, wrapped in his arms. I turn and face him, only to find the softest blue eyes staring at me.

"Seda, you're awake now. I came in here to give you a bath, and you were sleeping." He smiles. What do I say to him? I just smile back. Finally I find my voice.

"My table is broke."

"Baby, don't worry. When I'm done it will be like brand new. Are you ready for a bath?"

My eyes are blinking, because he's just taking over. I don't like it. I can bathe myself. I'm not surrendering to him. He disappeared for three days.

"I can make my own bath, Layern," I sigh. "This is not a happy ending for us, I'm not wanted in Kalin. This rule came from Queen Nala, who is your mother. Do you understand?"

"Yes, Seda, I understand."

"Thank you, so if you would leave and let me get over you..."

"I said I understand, not that I will give you up. I'm not going anywhere, in fact I've brought enough clothes to last me for a while."

"What do you mean?"

"I'm moving in, Seda. You got me every day, all day."

"You can't stay here. What the hell do I tell people?"

"You tell them your boyfriend moved in."

"This is getting out of hand. I'm really trying not to disrespect you, but-"

"First, say whatever you need. Second, just treat me normally, not as a prince, and third, I'm not leaving."

We stare at each other, and he quickly kisses me. My mouth opens slightly and his tongue enters. It's delicious. I pull away.

"What are you doing?"

"I'm trying to give you a bath, so I can fix the table."

"No, no, I'm talking about you, here on Earth, specifically with me."

"You let me worry about that, Seda, now bathe," he says. I'm lifted up and before he puts me into the bath, he blows heat into the water and I see steam. The bath feels good and I lean back, deciding to address later the issue of him moving in.

***

After I've dressed in some comfy shorts and a tank top. I walk downstairs, only to see that my kitchen table is put back together. Wow, that was fast, I think to myself. I find Layern in my office, on my computer, looking at all my business files. Ok, this is an invasion of privacy.

"Layern, get the hell away from my computer," I snap.

"Sorry, Seda, I was looking at your business. You do very well, I would like to see your shop tomorrow."

"NOOOO!!!"

He raises his brow and smiles slightly. I think he thinks this is funny.

"Problem?"

"Yes, you can't stay here, I'm not taking you to my shop." I take a deep breath. "You can't stop Palmer from coming over, either. You will have to go."

He shakes his head without a word. This is not happening. He's trying to take over my life.

"You need to relax, I'll get you some wine, and here, have a seat," he says, standing. I walk over and sit in my chair, glaring at him.

"Reseda Fire, you have such fire inside you. I'm going to enjoy living with you." He's gone before I can respond. I look at my computer; he has been looking at my products. Layern returns with two bottles of wine and two glasses.

"Layern, you can't come here and try to change my life."

"I'm not changing your life, well maybe a little, but you will like it."

"I already hate this. Please, why do you think you can stay with me?"

You don't like me?"

I stare at him in shock. This has nothing to do with whether I like him. I grab the bottle of wine and pour myself a full glass, drinking it non-stop. I pour myself another glass, turning towards the computer. I'm not even going to discuss the issue with him right now. He is determined to stay. I guess one night won't hurt. As I turn towards the clock, I notice it is three p.m. I can't believe the time. I begin working, and Layern sits down and watches my every move. Throwing myself into work, I order wax, scents and pre-made candles. That is the majority of my sales in my shop. I have other small items. My wealth, though, comes from being alive for three hundred and ten years. My father made sure that I will never want for money, plus I invest all the time.

"Do you make the candles?"

"Yes, I do."

"Hmm, would you make me some blue candles, you pick the scent."

"Umm, sure. I didn't think dragons would enjoy a scented candle."

"Why not?

I think about that for a second, and I really don't know.

"I'm not sure. It's not like I get a chance to be around dragons, so some things are from what I think."

"I'll teach you everything, Lecena."

"Thank you." I smile. Oh my, what is happening? Does he really like me? I'm pulled away from my thoughts as I hear knocking on the door. Shit, I know who that is, Palmer. Layern and I share a stare, and then a huge smile comes across his face.

"Well, Lecena, it's time for me to formally introduce myself."
This is going to get ugly.

LAYERN

Reseda and I both rush to the door, but I'm much faster than she is. I pull the door open and Palmer stands with eyes wide, and if I'm not mistaken, he gasps. He looks shocked and hurt. She winces a little, not knowing how to address this issue. The smile across my face says it all. Seda glares at me, which only makes me want her more. Folding my arms, I prepare to give Palmer exciting news.

"You are not allowed in our home any more. I will allow you to speak with my lecena, but nothing further."

"Fuck you, this is Reseda's home."

"I live here too, now." Seda comes and stands in front of me, trying to get my attention. I avoid eye contact, as this human male thinks he's coming in.

"FUCK YOU!" Palmer yells.

"I don't fuck men, but I will fuck you up if you yell at me one more time," I growl. Palmer steps back. I'm sure that frightened him.

Seda speaks."Layern, please give me and Palmer a moment."
I like the fire in her, my lecena is making me hot. I'm not leaving
though, it's not in my nature to submit to anyone, especially a
human.

"No, Seda."

"Seda? Her name is Reseda, asshole."

I glare at him and give him a small push on the shoulder,
which sends him flying down the stairs. I don't like anyone calling
me names. I'm sure he didn't know that, but now he does.

"Layern, stop!" Seda rushes after him. Palmer is halfway
down the steps and he looks pissed, but he's starting to get
annoying. Seda is even trying to make sure he's ok, I'll need to
talk to her about that. I know that my mother has me here for her
on mission, but I like Seda, and I'm here to get to know her. She
must know dragon males are very jealous, so I do hope she finds
her place next to me quickly.

"Seda?"

"Don't Seda me, Layern," she yells. "He's bleeding, you
bully. Listen, I might not control some things, but I'm not budging
on my friend. He's coming in and I'm going to make sure there is
no serious damage."

"Please, Seda, don't fight me on this."

"Layern," she snarls, "get the fuck out the way, or come help
me get him inside!"

I look into her eyes and see anger, but also a pleading lecena.

My eyes flash to Palmer, whose mouth is bleeding, and our eyes meet. He's very pissed and embarrassed, but that's not my concern, only Seda. I don't want to fight with her, but she wants this human to come in, who I know wants to fuck her. Shit! I walk over, take his left arm and pull him to his feet with little effort. I pull him into the house, stopping in the foyer, he doesn't need to come any further.

"Only for you, Seda," I say, calmly.

"Can you go get some ice?"

"No."

"Layern, please go get some ice and a towel, please."

I look at her in amazement, she's already had me let this human fucker in the house. I will not tend to him like a servant. "If I have to go get the ice-"

"You are going to go get the ice, Reseda," I say, through clenched teeth. I'm trying to be a gentleman, but Seda must not forget there's only so much I will take. She glares and storms off, leaving me with this unwanted guest. I take this time for my advantage; as Seda has a soft spot for him, I will be as kind as possible.

"Palmer, listen, I don't want you around her, you have a hidden agenda."

He looks up at me, hate in his eyes.

"I love her, and unless she tells me to stay away I will come to her door for the rest of my life."

"A short life you will have if you do."

"You going to kill me?" he says, holding his sore mouth. "How do you think Reseda will take that? I'm pretty sure she doesn't want a killer."

"I'm pretty sure she knows exactly who I am, Palmer."

Seda's back with some ice and a towel.

"Come on, Palmer, you need to lie down in the T.V. room."

I don't believe this, she's letting him come all the way in. Fuck! Our eyes meet as she walks him towards the room. I glare and she glares back, she and I will get some things straight tonight.

She takes care of him and he's eating up the attention, but I'm standing off to the side and watching, making sure she does the minimum. I'm getting upset at how attentive she is to him. My only thought is to throw his ass out of the house, but Seda would be pissed. He finally looks up at me.

"Feel better, little boy?" I ask.

"I feel great, there's nothing better than a beautiful woman taking good care of you," Palmer says.

Seda gives me a look, and though I've only been around for a little while, I knew she doesn't want me to say anything.

"Palmer, Layern and I are more than friends," Seda sighs. "You are still welcome to come over, but I think you should call first from now on, just until Layern gets used to you. You are still my very good friend."

Palmer looks at her and just nods, but I pick up that he is angry, and it's different. He wants to say something, but he holds back his words, and I can't get a good read on him. Humans can be so frustrating, especially when I can't read them. Palmer stands, says goodbye to Seda and leaves. Seda goes to the kitchen and starts cooking. I take a seat at the kitchen island; the table, though it's fixed, needs to rest with the liquid glues I used. It's not acceptable to use Kalin products on Earth, but I think this can be overlooked in the circumstances.

Seda is trying very hard to ignore me, but even in anger, her arousal is profound. I'm not used to a woman this angry at me. Saying sorry is not something I do, but I can give her some pleasure. Maybe that will change her mood.

"Lecena, you angry?" I ask, walking towards her. Seda's back is to me, but I can see her tense as I get close. She's blocking her feelings again, damn. I hate that she can do that so well.

"Layern," she snaps, "you can't come into my life and start kicking other people out of my life, who, by the way, have been around a lot longer than you."

"I'm not trying to kick people out of your life, but you do understand he's a human, right?"

"I'm half human, too. I have things in common with him, and he's been there for me... he was the only person around when my father died." She turns to me with a cold stare. "I grieved for my father by myself," she whispers, "until Palmer came along. Your mother banned me from even coming into Kalin, and I needed my mother."

If this guy Palmer is only a friend, maybe I have to ease up some. My mother can be a hardass, but she's my mother. I couldn't fathom not seeing her. Seda says her mother and my mother were best friends, how did that friendship end? That question I'll ask later, but for now my lecena needs some distraction, and so do I.

"Come, let me make you feel better," I say, holding my hand out to her. She looks at me, then turns off the stove, placing her small, soft, gentle hand in mine. The pain she feels comes from my mother. My heart bleeds for her, driving me to come up with some solution to end her pain at not being accepted. I pick her up and carry her to the bedroom.

"Layern, thank you."

"For what, Seda?"

She doesn't answer, and right now I only want to bury myself in her sweet, sweet pie. I fall to my knees in front of her, placing my hands on her hips, gripping her shorts at the waist. My body is hurting. I want her so badly, but slow is what she needs right now. She's wearing panties again. Oh, when will she learn? My decision to rip her shorts off is not planned, but her wearing panties just gets to me. I'm going to take them off whenever she's wearing them. Grinning to myself, I position my head right at her sex, pressing my lips against her panties. Seda places a leg over my shoulder and steadies herself with her hands in my hair, pulling hard. "Mmmm," screaming is what she needs.

As I slide her panties to the side, my tongue slithers into her glistening sex. My hair gets pulled harder, so she must like that. My hands grip her afla and I open wide. Her sex, panties and her orgasm are in my mouth as I suck and bite her. She moans loudly,

"Ahh, mmm!" Her leg shakes on my shoulder and I know she's coming again. I rip the panties this time, taking them from my mouth and placing them in my back pocket. Quickly I place her on the floor and spread her legs wide, and she's twisting under me and her eyes change from human to beast. I don't waste any time, pulling her top off and bending to capture her nipples as her body moves under me. Her hips thrust forward, an invitation to enter her body. I take her offer, diving right in, and our bodies are in rhythm. Each thrust is better than the last. My thighs are dripping with her juices, and she's like a river overflowing onto me. We can't stay in this position for long, as our beasts are enjoying each other as well, and need to be moved often. I pull her up into a sitting position and she takes over, sliding her silky, sweaty body up and down my sex, with an occasional twist. Seda feels so good, my hands are in her hair pulling, while my body begs for more.

"Seda, baby,"

"Mmmm, yes," she moans. Seda is tormenting me with her pace, slow and deadly, and to get her back, I swiftly flip her over onto her hands and knees, pushing back inside. My pace increases and I feel my release coming.

I bend, whispering in her ear, "Scream for me, baby." That's all it takes and she's screaming until her body is convulsing and I follow her with my own release, muttering her name. We fall asleep on our sides, still connected. I think I could get used to this.

***

After Seda and I wake and take a long hot shower, making love a couple more times in the shower, I decided to take her out to dinner. She is reluctant at first, but she soon agrees. I want to take her some place nice so that she will have to dress up, so I make reservations at Commander's Palace, one of the best restaurants in town. I am dressed a lot faster than Reseda.

"Layern, can you please tell me why we are going out to eat, they are not going to serve you enough food," she says, pulling up her white lace panties. My head cocks to the side as I wonder why she continues to wear them, she's half dragon, don't they bother her, or has she not noticed my obsession with them? I love having the smell of her in my pocket, it's fucking amazing!

"What color dress you wearing?"

"I decided to wear a yellow one."

"I think I want you in the navy blue halter, with the split in the front."

"Oh."

"Oh." I mock her words back. Seda blushes, but returns with the dress I want on her. I have plans for her tonight, and this dress is going to give me easy access.

RESEDA

This day started off great, the mess with Palmer and Layern still needs to be addressed, but dinner out tonight sounds good. It's like a date. I've only been on two dates in my life, and they both ended badly. I hope tonight will be different. Layern calls me his girl, but I'm not sure he's my guy. Queen Nala is a force that just doesn't stop, and I'm not strong enough ever to come up against her. I didn't realize he had a car with him until we walked out and I saw a sea- blue Camaro. It's decked out with rims and tint. The Draglen brothers can have a chauffeur drive them. Why would a prince want to drive?

"Layern, when did you get your car?"

"I always keep a car in big cities, Seda, why?"

"I mean, you are a billionaire on Earth, they usually don't drive around in a Camaro."

"Lecena, I'm not your average billionaire, you know dragons

are independent, besides I'll never have a safety issue."

"I'm sure you won't," I smile.

He parks on a side street near Commander's Palace. I'm sure he knows they have valet parking, why are we going to walk half a block away? I didn't know we were coming here, but the closer we got, the more I figured out where he was taking me. It's nice outside. The sun is going down and it's actually a romantic gesture. We walk holding hands. This is a first for me. Never in my three hundred and ten years have I walked down the street holding a man's hand. Well, he's a dragon.

"Layern why are you being so, so... boyfriendish?"

"'Boyfriendish' is not a word on Earth or Kalin, Seda." He smiles.

"I know, but you understand what I'm talking about. Why do you want me, knowing your mother will have my head if she finds out?"

He shakes his head in disbelief, frowning. I didn't mean to bring up his mother, but she's been a constant threat to me. I can't just drop this.

"You're a beautiful woman, Seda. I love your red hair, your soft, pale skin, the way your plump, pretty lips wrap around my sex." He stops walking. "I never thought I would want to get to know another, but you spark something inside me I can't explain. So, if you're worrying about my mother, I'll protect you no matter what. I don't want you living in fear any more, ok?"

Well, I didn't expect all that. I take his hand and start walking again. I didn't expect him to get so deep, but I will never allow him to turn against his family for me, I'm not worth it. We finally arrive at the restaurant and take our seats.

"Layern," I say, smiling, "it's not going to be polite for us to order four meals apiece. I do believe people will stare."

"Order whatever you want, Seda."

The waiter approaches. She's in her mid-twenties with black, pixie-cut hair, green eyes and a beautiful smile. I dislike her instantly. She proves my feelings right, smiling at Layern and ignoring the fact that I'm sitting with him. Layern smiles back after placing the order, but as she walks away, my beast lets out a very low growl, stopping her dead in her tracks. She turns and looks at me, and I give her a small nod. She moves quickly into the back.

"Don't flirt with her," I snap.

"I wasn't flirting, Seda."

"I can get real jealous, and very ugly, if you smile at her like that again."

"How did I smile?"

"Don't play fucking games. I'm not in control of myself if I get too pissed, so tread lightly."

"There's that fire I love about you, Reseda Fire."

"Don't make fun."

He smiles at me, then places one finger over his mouth. "Mmm," I moan out loud. His mouth is very distracting. My eyes focus on his lips. He takes his napkin from the table and drops it on the floor. What is he doing? He pushes away from the table and goes quickly under the tablecloth, and before I can think, I feel his hot hands going up my dress, pulling at my panties. I raise my hips so he can get at them, and he slowly moves them down my legs. I shift in my seat, as he's just got me all hot in a restaurant full of people. I look around, noticing other couples looking at me, which makes me more uncomfortable.

"Layern, people are looking." He comes up with my panties in his hand, oh no, I thought he would have put them away in his pocket. Our eyes meet and my head is shaking, this is not happening in a public place.

"Smell so good, Lecena," he says, smelling my panties. Oh my, why is this so hot?

"Please," I beg, softly.

"Shhh." He lays my panties where the napkin was, neatly placing his silverware on top of them, oh God, I'm going to pass out right here.

"Please take my panties off the table," I whisper.

"No, you think I want someone else. That I was flirting? Seda, I really want to place your firm afla on top of the table and eat my dessert now." I shift in my seat, my body aching for him. I can't orgasm at the table, Reseda, get yourself together, I say in my head. I see the waitress heading towards us with salads, oh she's going to see my panties on the table.

"Layern, please take them off the table."

"No, Lecena." He smiles. The waitress comes smiling, and puts down my salad, and as she turns to place his plate down, she notices my panties. Her eyes are wide and she makes eye contact with me and she's blushing, I'm blushing, and Layern is smiling, enjoying my embarrassment. The waitress is so stunned, she's standing there looking at my panties. Layern takes it further and picks up his salad fork, wiping it off with the crotch of my panties. I'm dreaming, please let me be dreaming. He starts eating his salad, and the waitress runs back to the kitchen.

"Mmmm, this is the best salad I've ever had, Seda. You should eat, you look a little pale." He smirks. This is not funny, he needs to give me back my panties.

"Layern, can you please give me my panties back?"

"No, and you should eat, we are going to have a long night, Lecena."

"Take my panties off the fucking table!" I yell. He looks at me cocking his head to the side, making it very hard to be serious when he's so damn sexy. He slowly puts down his fork. Picking up my panties, he dabs the corners of his mouth, sending my libido into overdrive.

"If you don't eat, you will want to sleep tonight, and I'm not tired, I missed a couple of spots to suck on you, so please, EAT!" He growls the last word.

My nipples stand to attention with his words. Slowly, I take the fork in my hand and put some salad in my mouth. I'm not sure if I even taste food. Layern's words have me wanting to leave the food and go straight home. How did I fall so quickly?

"Dragons fall faster for each other. We are not bound by rules.

You are usually hard to read, but that came through clearly." He grins.

We eat in silence through salad and our entrée. The waitress comes with the last course, dessert. She sets down two pieces of lemon pie. I'm not a huge fan of lemon pie, but I will take a bite or two. Really, my interest is to get home and see what spots he's missed. I grin to myself.

"Layern, I'm not a huge fan of lemon pie, but I will try a couple of bites, ok?"

He gives me the sexiest look ever, I mean ever. I could get on the table myself for him at this moment.

"Oh baby, I love pie, any type of pie, I'm missing one thing, though."

"What?"

He smiles.

"Can you do me a favor?"

"I'm not sure. What do you want?"

"Can you take two fingers and insert them inside you?"

Oh my, I'm not doing that, Layern is out of his mind. I'm starting to think he would like to fuck me in public, with people around. I'm so in shock I just shake my head, that's not happening.

"Do it, Seda, or I will."

"Layern, I'm not doing that," I whisper.

"Please, just this one time." He pouts. I can't believe this! He's pouting like a child. Would he really do it? We are in a staring contest, but I soon get lost in his blue eyes, with the split in front, maybe it could work without anyone knowing.

"Yes?"

"Layern, only this time."

"Use your right hand and place your left on the table."

"Why?"

"So I can hold your hand."

I don't question that. I just place my left hand on the table, and he quickly puts his hand over the top of mine. My entire body begins to warm. I don't need any help. I've been about to burst the entire dinner. My right hand moves up my thigh and my legs open, giving me better access. My fingers find my folds, and just doing this out in public is so erotic.

"Seda, go on, push them inside," Layern whispers.

I want to roll my eyes into the back of my head, but my fingers slide in with ease. It feels so good. Layern is watching me intensely. My eyes widen. I can hear the sound of my juices as I push in and out. "Mmmm," I moan softly.

"That's enough, Seda, pull them out and offer me your fingers."

Oh, I can't, my fingers are wet. Layern is so nasty. He has no shame. He squeezes my hand hard, and I shake my head, continuing to pleasure myself, His stare is intense and I pull my fingers out, leaving my body aching, and raise them to the side of my plate.

Layern moves faster than the human eye, and has my fingers in his mouth sucking hard. My sex begins to ache for him, and my mouth goes slack and I'm resisting the urge to throw my head back and orgasm right in front of everyone. Layern can make you forget about everything. I watch him eat his pie. Pie is not what I want. I need him inside me now! He finally finishes, and we pay and begin our walk back to the car.

***

Night is upon us now, and we take our time walking and holding hands. The electricity between us is thick, and undeniably pleasurable. It only makes me want Layern more. My mind can only see both of our bodies naked, kissing, sucking, licking, and biting. Layern glances at me. We make it to the car and I think we are getting in, but Layern pushes me against the wall and pulls my dress up, and my ass is on the cold wall.

"I thought I could wait, but knowing you are not wearing any panties, and tasting that sweet pie you have, I need you now."

I'm panting so loud, I'm surprised I can hear him. We are all over each other. His hands are in my hair and my hands are gripping his sex.

"Layern, don't tease me."

"Oh Lecena, I'm not."

My legs are wrapped around his waist and he quickly unbuttons his pants and his erection is free. Yes is my thought. I want him and he responds, pushing himself inside, and with all the play at the restaurant, screaming in pleasure is amazing. Our flesh on flesh is all I focus on. If anyone walks by I don't care, I want this. I need this. Layern's hand slams against the wall next to my head, and I'm sure I feel crumbling rocks falling.

"Oh yessss!" I moan.

He stops and slides out enough that he can see his sex drenched in my juices.

"Damn, I love the sight of me covered with you," he whispers.

We continue, and soon find our release together. I'm not sure how long we are up against the wall, but after Layern carries me to the car, I notice his handprint in the wall. We left our mark. Wow!

LAYERN

It's only been a week, and Seda and I are doing great. Palmer has only attempted to stop by once, and Seda talked with him on the porch. She's starting to understand my feelings about Palmer. I respect hers as best I can about their relationship. It's only a matter of time before I'm required to give my mother some information, and at dinner I decide to start searching for some.

"Seda, this gumbo is quite tasty, where did you learn to cook?"

"My father taught me, I mean it wasn't like I had a mother around to bake cookies with," she says, calmly. I'm not happy about asking questions she's not comfortable about, but given an order from Queen Nala, you never have an option to say no.

"Your father did a good job."

"He was the best dad a girl could want. Let's not talk about me, tell me more about you."

Shit, the conversation is not about me, but I have no choice.

"What would you like to know?"

"Your gift, Cortamagen, everything. I'm so out of touch with dragon life."

"My gift is called joha, and it's not always a gift." I sigh. "It can be frustrating always knowing other people's feelings or their moods. It's not exact, but I'm almost always right. Well, as for Cortamagen, it's the most beautiful place ever. There's color everywhere, the trees are like skyscrapers, and the food is healthy and carries no health risks like humans have here on Earth."

"Hey, I'm human too."

"Yes, but dragon is your dominant. Do you want to know, or are you going to defend your Earthly ways?"

"Layern, yes, I want to know, continue, please."

I smile, watching her face light up about Cortamagen.

"It's the best place in Kalin, and also the largest, I'm sure you know that part, but the people are kind, and I love it."

"Why are you here, then?" she asks, with sorrow in her voice.

"I'm here because, although all that is in Cortamagen, I want you more."

This conversation is revealing too much about my feelings, damn!

"Layern, I like you, but I can't come to Cortamagen with you, ever. I'm not wanted there, although humans are welcomed into the castle." The words leave her mouth through clenched teeth. Yes, two of my brothers' Wellas are human, that wasn't accepted by the people at first, but things are great now. For the first time since I've met Seda, her guard is down, and I get flashes and feelings of her loneliness, anger, and betrayal, all directed at not being accepted in Kalin. How can my mother do this to such an innocent female dragon?

"Listen, I'm not sure why my mother banned you, but like I said before, I will always keep you safe."

"I'm banned because it's a punishment to my mother and my deceased father," she says, sternly. She rises from the table, walks over to the sink, and begins to cry. I stand, not really knowing what to do about her crying, but I have my arms around her and let her cry. Her feelings are blocked again, I can't get a read on why she's crying. My mother can be cruel, but I would never think she would forbid a dragon to enter our land.

Seda walks away from me and I follow. She climbs into bed and cries herself to sleep. I hold her until I know she's resting. I make my way downstairs, only to be greeted by three of my brothers: Gemi, Warton, and Domlen.

"Mother would like a report," Gemi says. They all walk into the kitchen and start helping themselves to food.

"I've only been here a week," I respond.

"Well, you've had enough time to fuck her good," Warton says smirking, "so you should know some information. Queen Nala is not happy." I've fought him numerous times, and only won maybe once or twice, yet I would like to punch him at this moment.

"Warton, why the hell did you come?" I growl, "you hate Earth."

"Our mother wanted me to come, in case you get brave, brother."

"Warton, one day I'm going to fuck you up."

"It will not be today, though."

I look at Gemi and Domlen and they are eating, getting a little too comfortable. Warton gets himself a mixing bowl of gumbo and sits on the countertop. That brother has some serious anger issues.

"I'm still working," I say, "so I have no news for you currently."

"Well, you need to get something from her," Domlen says, "before our mother makes good on her promise." I know he's right, but Seda has not told me anything, except that our mother is evil.

"I'll get something soon," I say, "but you can't be here. Besides, I'm not sharing bedroom shows with any of you." I can tell Domlen and Gemi would like to see Seda and me having sex. My brothers and I always share information, including showing one another a female as we bed her, except if we intend something more permanent, like a Giver or Wella. Although we do sometimes share Givers.

"Well, Layern, I know it's only been a week," Domlen says calmly, "but you need to give us something to take back."

They're hiding something, I can feel it. I don't like this sneaky shit. I stand still and get a read on the secret. Oh, she wants me away from Seda soon. I search hard, but my talented mother has blocked me from knowing more. My brothers don't truly know why, either. Seda did mention that her being banned is a punishment to her parents, not her. If that's the case, then Queen Nala has a secret, which she wants to stay hidden. Maybe I can help Seda out after all. I need more time, though.

"I can tell you that she loved her dad, and that he died ten years ago, that's all I have right now," I say. My brothers all look at me, then nod and continue eating.

They finally finish eating, and I assume they are leaving. That's when I realize they are here for a few days. My mother sure does know how to spoil a good thing. Warton is the first to speak.

"How many rooms does this half-breed have?"

"Warton, I'm not going to keep letting shit go. I can always open my mouth and tell your secrets."

"Ok, let's not make this any more unpleasant," Gemi says. "We are only here for one night, brother. If you would be so kind as to show us a place to rest, we are all tired. The portal can be draining, as you know."

"Yes, it's room for one night only." I growl. " She has five bedrooms, so it will be easy to accommodate you. Only for one night."

Domlen doesn't say a word. He goes in search of a room, and Warton follows, shaking his head at me. That asshole is so damn cocky. Gemi stays behind.

I walk into the library and take a seat in a comfortable chair. I know Gemi has stayed behind to talk.

"Layern, are you falling for this female?"

"I like her, brother, but love, I'm not sure. I don't trust any woman with my heart anymore."

"Well, if you are falling in love, I'm not against you. Love is what I have been wanting for a long time. I think, though, that if she finds out you are here for other reasons, it could end badly."

"Queen Nala knows how to fuck up a situation. You know if I would like to pursue love with Reseda, it's not possible. Our mother wants information, and then more than likely would like nothing better than to rip her to shreds."

"So what's your plan?"

"I plan on feeding Queen Nala as little information as possible until I can get Reseda out of her death sentence, because no matter what, she's going to die if I leave her side."

"I agree. If you need help…"

"I know, you are on my side."

Gemi leaves to find a room to rest, and I go and climb into bed with Seda. It feels so good to be next to her. She's resting peacefully, but after all the talk with my brothers I just need to be inside her. I wrap my arm around her waist, pressing her back to my chest, only to get a whiff of her sweet arousal. My hand slides up her t-shirt, finding her nipples. They are already hard for me. She moans, "Mmmm," as I gently pull on them.

"Lecena, wake up." I should block my brothers from seeing, but if Warton hears he will want to see, not because he cares, but only to see if I have serious feelings for her. He would not tell our mother like Hawken, but I would catch hell. Shit!

"Mmm, baby, don't you get tired?" she whispers. Her voice is sleepy and I should let her rest, but my other head is ruling me right now.

"Can I have just a small taste?" I ask, positioning myself between her legs.

"Umm, are you even giving me a choice?"

"Yes, Lecena, it's always a choice." She gives me a big smile with her eyes closed, nodding yes. I lower my head and softly kiss her lips, coaxing her to open her mouth, and she does, giving me a taste of her. I begin to kiss, suck and bite her everywhere, her neck, shoulders, nipples, navel, hips, thighs and I finally hit her sweet pie. It's like having the best dessert ever.

"Oh... please... Layern."

"Mmmm... where do you want my mouth, Lecena?"

Seda's body squirms under me, her panting is getting louder and I don't want anyone to hear now. I close out my brothers, and I feel Gemi and Warton both trying to enter my head to see. Domlen does not really care, he's seen and done a lot.

"I want your mouth, all over my cookie jar." I slide two fingers inside and she's clenching my fingers for life. I'm stuck on the fact that she just called her comfort zone her 'cookie jar'. I chuckle, amazing!

I place her legs on my shoulders so I can have good access. She smells delightful. My tongue enters her and she loses self-control. She's pushing my head hard against her. I suck every drop of her juices that comes out, getting my fill of her. I can't hold back any longer. Crawling up her body like the predator I am, I keep her legs on my shoulders and I'm inside her, building her back up to orgasm, with me this time. I watch her face and she's red as fire, and the enjoyment inside me is profound. We soon find our release together, both moaning in pleasure. Sex has always been the best part of life to me, but sex with Seda is fucking unbelievable. She takes me to places my mind thought could not exist anymore.

Sleep overtakes us both, soon after the best orgasm I've had in a very long time.

RESEDA

My eyes open slightly, then close again. I need a break, Layern is insatiable, and he's always horny. I've heard that Draglen brothers are big on sex and that Layern has it bad, but damn. I'm really sore and tired. I hear him breathing next to my ear. It's the most comforting thing ever. I can't believe I have a boyfriend and he's a dragon. It feels so good to be myself around him. There's no hiding my eyes when I'm angry, and most of all, I get to learn more about Kalin, my real home. I move a little, only to realize Layern has me in a grip that's almost deathly. I try to move his arm and push his leg off me, but he tightens up.

"Where you going?"

"Its morning, and I have to pee. You don't have to pee?"

"I already have, just didn't want you to try and run."

Why would he think I would run? He doesn't move, just lies holding me. What's his problem? Then I hear them, dragons in my kitchen. I turn to look at him, and he squeezes me tighter.

"Listen, if we are real quiet, maybe they will eat and just go."

"Who's in my kitchen?"

"A few of my brothers."

"WHAT?"

"Shhh, you're going to-"

He stops speaking and I hear footsteps at the door. They're not going to just open the door, oh please, I'm naked.

"Layern, we know you and the female are awake. We're hungry. Come eat breakfast, brother."

"Oh, we will eat later," Layern responds.

"We want to meet her, Layern."

The brother walks away and I turn and stare at Layern, my eyes saying it all. I'm nervous, angry and scared.

"That was my brother Domlen, he's demanding sometimes, but a really good dragon, I don't think they are leaving until they see you," he says, apologetically.

"My house is full of Draglen brothers?"

"No only three are here, and with me that makes four, not many at all."

I have no words. I try to move and my body really lets me know how sore I am. I wince, knowing my cookie jar will be extremely sore too. I will not be having any wild sex with Layern for at least a day.

"I will run some bath water for you, Lecena, my brothers will wait."

I look at him, hoping that his brothers will leave. I like Layern being around, but his brothers? I'm not sure how they'll respond to my being half dragon. He doesn't say a word, just rises and goes to the bathroom, running water for a bath. He stays in there for a few minutes, and soon I smell something sweet. Layern comes back and picks me up without a word, and soon we are both in the water. He seems distracted. I'm not sure why his mood has changed, but it's different. After we bathe, we dress and I prepare to meet his brothers. My hands are sweaty, damn!

"Well, you finally came out of the room, brother," Gemi says, smiling. The others' eyes are on me, and though this is my house and my kitchen, I feel out of place. I sway from foot to foot, then finally I go to the table where a feast has been set out. The food has not been touched; they truly did wait for us.

"Seda, come, let's have breakfast," Layern says, pulling me to the table. I sit next to Gemi and Layern sits next to me. My table is round and seats six people, but these brothers are too big for it. I smile to myself, looking at them all at my table.

"Something funny?" one brother asks. This brother is tall and slender, very handsome with blond hair, and dressed all in black. He looks very intimidating, his eyes are narrow and there is no emotion in his face.

I find my voice, "Yes, something is funny, but it's private." My father always said that if I showed fear, then it would be looked on as a weakness, and dealing with dragons, weakness is not acceptable. Besides, this is my house.

"Warton," Layern says, a warning in his voice. Warton is his name, I've read about him and seen some pictures of him in books my father gave me. According to the books, Warton is the best warrior, but he's not friendly.

"Layern, I simply asked a question, no harm, right Reseda?" He keeps his eyes on Layern. I pull Layern's hand into mine, as I can tell he's getting angry.

"No harm, Warton, let's just have breakfast," I say.

"We will fix our plates after you, Reseda." I'm sure that's Domlen.

They have fixed all sorts of food, from bacon to steaks. There's even grits on the table. I start fixing my plate and they wait very patiently for me to finish. Then they start making plates, and when they are done, all the food is gone. We all eat in silence and I realize that this must be some tradition or something.

"Do you all always eat in silence?" I whisper to Layern.

"Yes, we do, Reseda, it's hard to explain, but we talk when we're at home in Cortamagen. Have you ever been?" Domlen asks.

"I do believe she was talking to me, brother," Layern snaps.

"Yes, I answered for you and now I'm waiting on her response, brother. We do have to go home soon."

Layern eyes flicker from soft blue to a deep dark blue, he looks like a dragon shifter ready to attack in my kitchen. This is not good.

"I've never been to Cortamagen, not because I have no desire, but only because your mother, Queen Nala, has banned me." I glare. Why are his brothers here? Layern never spoke of them coming. Did the Queen send them? Gemi stands, taking out his portal.

"It's time to go, Domlen, Warton," he says.

Layern stands and after a nod to each other, the brothers vanish into their portals. I can't believe I have just been in the presence of some of the greatest dragons ever. Although that Warton is an ass and I agree with Layern, Domlen is demanding. I like Gemi. I glance at Layern and he's still standing, both hands clenched and a serious look on his face. Something is wrong and he's not sharing it with me. Maybe it has to do with home.

"Layern, I'm going into my store today. Make yourself at home," I say, rising. I begin taking plates, bowls and glasses to the sink. Dishes are piling up in both sinks.

"Work?"

"Yes, work, Layern. I can't stay in bed with you all the time."

"Why?" He relaxes, and gives me a sexy smile. No, I'm not going to get pulled back into bed with this very hot guy. He's tempting, but no, sex is not everything.

"I'm going to work, you can stay and relax, and I'll be home late this afternoon."

"Oh, I guess I'm coming to work with you, then."

"Oh no, you can't. I'm friends with the other business owners on the block, and you... you are distracting."

"I will stay behind the counter and watch you, I promise, but if you think I'm leaving your side, you are mistaken."

"Layern, I'm not going to run away."

"I know, but I'm still going."

I take a deep breath and march straight to my room, snatching out a summer dress, tossing it on the bed and picking out some panties and a bra to wear, as well. From the bed, Layern smirks at me.

"If you're going you need to get dressed, you can't walk around with just some sleep pants with no shirt and shoes."

"Why are you angry?"

I turn to look at him, and instantly my body responds. I don't try to speak. I just continue to get ready. Layern decides to wear some casual slacks and a polo shirt, with sandals. After much discussion I find myself in Layern's car. We pull around back to my shop.

"What's the name of your shop?"

"Fire Candles and More," I say, proudly.

He doesn't ask anything else. We walk in, and my shop looks small with him in here. Layern takes it upon himself to walk through. I see him picking up and smelling my little items. This seems like a dream. I'm sleeping with a Draglen brother, and he's at my store, picking up my items.

I turn on all the things that need to be on, lighting some candles and clicking on the sign outside that says 'OPEN'. While I am checking the cash register, I notice Layern sitting in a chair, just watching me, not saying anything. My heart starts to beat a little faster. He makes me feel alive. My father would not be happy with this - me sleeping not only with a dragon, but Queen Nala's son. This could cost me my life. I look into his eyes, though, and I hope this doesn't end my life or my mother's.

"Stop thinking so hard, Seda, I will keep you safe, and your mother."

I look up from counting, and taking a deep breath, I continue. My stress level is rising. Maybe I should end this with Layern. My mother's life is important to me, and having great sex does not take precedence over it.

"Layern, I…"

"No, stop, don't think about that," he says. I spot a couple coming close to the door, and so does Layern. He moves quickly behind the counter, which is pretty high because I'm tall. The counter is wooden, and no one can see him but me. I gasp, knowing he's going to do something distracting. The door opens, and in walks a beautiful older couple. They are Black, and look to be in their sixties.

"Well, good morning, darlin," the lady says. I've never seen them in my shop before, but she's excited.

"Good morning, ma'am. Can I help you find something in particular?"

"Oh no, I just want to look, and pick up a few of your candles. My sister raves about them, and Mr. Helms promised me candles." She smiles at, I assume, her husband. He looks around and I just smile at how happy she looks. It's not long before big, hot hands are sliding up my dress.

"AH!" I yell.

"You ok?" the lady asks, and I just nod. She starts humming, and Layern slides my panties to the side, inserting a finger. *Oh My.* The warmth of his finger inside me is pleasurable, but painful, because I'm at work and have to try and keep my face normal.

"Yes, MA'AM!" I squeal, as Layern starts licking my inner thigh.

Her husband looks at me strangely, and I start fumbling around with papers trying to get away from Layern, but he bites me hard, stilling me. My lip is going to be raw, as hard as I'm sucking it. I feel him get onto his knees, and though people are in my shop, I open my legs wider. I want him. His hands find my ass and he squeezes hard and places his mouth on my sex, sucking my folds through my panties. This is so unprofessional, but he's sucking me through my panties and I don't want him to stop.

"What kind of scent is this?" the woman asks. "I can't tell." I want to speak, but words have failed me, Layern has now pressed just the tip of his pinky finger into my ass. I bend over like I'm in pain, but really I want to scream out in pleasure, it feels good. I mean it's foreign, but the foreplay is so intense and I'm so wet that it doesn't hurt.

"Ummm... its... oh.... that's CALLED, Cherry Pine!" I finally spit out. I'm making a fool out of myself, but right now, my sexual side is outweighing all of my logical sense.

"You sure you're ok?"

"Yes," I whimper.

He moves his finger in and out, and then pushes a finger into my sex, I don't know which way to push, forwards or backwards, my body doesn't know how to react to all this. Layern is so wrong, he's got me at work looking crazy.

"Ok, I think I've got everything," the nice woman says. Her husband comes and pays. My hands are trembling, I'm slurring my words. Layern's not showing any mercy. The couple finally leaves and I use my mind to lock the door and shut off the 'open' sign light, something I've not done in years.

"Ohhhhh… please!" I beg.

"Open your legs wider," he commands.

I do as I'm told, pulling my dress up by the sides to see his face. "Oh," his tongue comes out of his mouth and he starts sucking my clitoris. The scream that comes from me is all beast: "Ahhhggrrrrr".

"Don't talk about stopping this anymore, Seda." He speaks so calmly against my sex. I whimper more, my legs are getting weak. I'm going to orgasm, and it's only a few seconds later that I explode all over his fingers and face. I can hear him slurping up my juices. This is so nasty. I feel ashamed, but I can't stop myself.

My panties are ripped off, and I've decided I'm not wearing panties around him anymore. I look down and with one hand he's gripping my ass, with the other hand he's unbuttoning his slacks, I can't wait, bending down with trembling hands I finish unbuttoning his slacks and freeing his erection. I haven't had my chance to suck him, not even sure if I'm any good at it, but I want a taste. My mouth is around him and instinct kicks in and I begin to suck and pull hard. I hear him panting now.

His hands are now in my hair and his hips are thrusting forward, pumping my mouth with such a force, my lips starts aching. He swings my body around and now my sex is in his face and he's sucking me as I'm doing him.

"Baby, wait, I need you to climb on top and ride me."

I don't speak, I let go of his sex, turning my body, positioning myself on top of him. I feel his erection at my entrance and I slide down. It takes me a minute to adjust, but I'm soon in a rhythm with him, my hands under his shirt as I go up and down, round and round. Pulling up all the way to the tip and slamming down. Oh, wow, he feels so good. I never knew sex could be this good. We make love right there behind the counter my in shop for, I'm sure, a couple of hours.

***

My hair is a mess. I'm in the back with a brush, trying to untangle it, when Layern comes in and watches me from behind.

"We can't do that again. You are not allowed behind the counter, ever." I smile.

"Really? Why? You had fun, right?" He raises a brow at me.

"It's not happening again, and I look a mess now."

"You look perfect, and I love that red hair, Seda."

I bite the inside of my cheek, my lips are too sore and I need something to bite. As I'm fixing my dress, ensuring I look appropriate for work, he smoothes out the back of my dress, making sure he lingers over my butt. We smile at each other in the mirror, and it feels so good to have him around, and not just because the sex is awesome.

The rest of the day is normal. Layern stays off to the side watching me, and is always on his feet when a man comes into the store. I think he's jealous. I smile, and reality hits me. I may want to pursue more with Layern, but Queen Nala will never allow it. I'll just have fun with Layern for now. He's so honest and would never hurt me. I can see that now.

LAYERN

I attacked Seda in her store, without even thinking. My brothers this morning had me pissed. Especially Warton's angry afla. Then she puts on panties in front of me getting ready, and to top it off my mother is asking me to give her information quickly. She has no intention of letting Seda live, I see that. I'm not sure how to prevent it from happening. Her sending Warton is a warning for me if I get in the way. I'm not strong enough to stop my mother, but I have to figure out how if I can get clever. I'm not in love with Seda, I just care deeply for her. Queen Nala should know that. My father, King Dramen, should see that love is not what I want. I just like her company. I can't make her a Giver because she's a little too feisty for that title. Seda is going to hate me when she finds out I had to get information to send back to my mother; but I will keep her safe.

Seda and I are watching a movie called 'A Time to Kill.' I had never heard of the movie before, but I believe it's always a time to kill. I've killed numerous times and it was always necessary. She's so into this movie. I'm thinking about how to keep her alive, for Queen Nala is persistent on her missions.

"Layern, this movie makes me cry every time I watch it, that poor child," she says.

I pull her closer, hoping I can protect her, because I'm sure that there's a fire coming for her. If only I can get the secret out of her, I can use it against my mother. Maybe that could help save her.

***

The next three days are heavenly. I follow her to her job and I contain my sexual advances, mostly. Nothing she can't handle. We plan a night of dancing, and then she tells me she wants Palmer to come.

"I don't want him to think I'm not a good friend." She glares. I chuckle, her glaring is sexy. I just want to bed her every time she does it.

"He really likes you, Seda, the reason why the male human has stayed away is because his feelings are very strong toward you," I say.

"I don't care," she snarls. "He has been my friend for ten years. I haven't known you for ten weeks. I'm not dropping my friend. I don't care how good the sex is." I can't speak because I'm pissed. I take a couple of deep breaths. She says she doesn't care how good the sex is! Well, she will beg me before I give another orgasm to her. This is why I will never take a Wella. Things were good, but she has to be stubborn.

"Invite him," I say, calmly. She doesn't need to know how she's wounded me with her words. True I've not known her long, but we dragons are not bound by human laws. Our beasts become familiar, and that's good enough.

"Ok, I will."

She picks up the phone and I tune in, clearly hearing what he says too.

"Hey, Palmer."

"What? You're allowed to call me?"

"It's not like that... would you like to go dancing with us tonight?"

I can hear him laugh. Fucker.

"I'm not going anywhere with your hulk. He doesn't know anything about manners, Reseda."

"We are not talking about him, ok? I want to see you."

She glances at me. I narrow my eyes and she narrows hers back. This has to stop.

"Listen, you're my friend, and you said you always would be. So, if you don't mind, we will be at the same place as last time in about an hour."

"I really don't want to deal with that guy again,"

"I'll dance with you."

"Really?"

"Yes!"

"Ok. I will be there, but keep your pit bull on a leash."

She laughs, she thinks that's funny. Ok!

"Bye, Palmer."

"Thanks, Reseda. I missed my friend. See you tonight."

She hangs up the phone, folds her arms and stares at me. I stalk towards her, bending so that we are nose to nose. I can't believe my anger.

"If you think you're dancing with him, you're going to get that human hurt, Seda," I hiss.

"Layern, it's only a dance. You can't get jealous over a dance."

"Seda, my lecena, please don't make me hurt him."

"Why are you?"

"Please don't make this a bad night."

"Wow, Prince Layern, any other demands I must do?"

I walk away and pour myself some homemade liquor that I bought from a guy in the city. I can't allow that disrespect, she may think its innocent, but Palmer-fucker wants her as his lady full time. I drink the entire glass down. She's behind me in no time, but I'm trying to calm myself.

"Layern?"

"Oh, I thought it was Prince Layern?" I snap. My back is to her and I feel her anger, also there's fear there as well. She thinks I would leave because of my anger?

"Why is this such a big deal?"

"Seda, it's a big deal. Please don't dance with him. I will get angry. I'm not backing down from this."

"I'm not going to back down, either. So, what does this mean?"

I turn and look into those beautiful orange eyes.

"It means we are going dancing, and if you attempt to dance with that human man, I won't apologize for what comes after."

Seda narrows her eyes at me and I just smile, but I'd really like to rip Palmer's head off now. Instead, I make a quick call home.

"I need you here to keep me from killing a human. You better bring reinforcements," I bark.

Seda's eyes are wide and I can feel she's considering changing her mind, but her stubbornness is outweighing her logic.

"Well, the only one that is available is Hawken," Gemi says.

"Fuck, I guess he will have to do, but I hope I don't have to burn his ass either."

"I'll see if I can convince another to come, but until then, no hurting humans. What time?"

"One hour."

"Ok."

I close the phone and she's staring at me with her mouth open, damn sexy mouth. I don't like arguing with her, but this is something I'm not bending on. I smile and blow her a kiss, she just turns and goes to get ready.

***

The ride to the dance bar is quiet. I decide to put some music on. Soon the car is filled with Stevie Wonder's soulful voice. Reseda smiles, because we share a love for music and dancing. I glance over and sing some of the lyrics.

"All I dooo, is think about you," I sing.

She joins in, and soon she's smiling. Maybe she will see it my way, and won't test me on this Palmer thing. We pull up and I see a Black SUV. I smile, thinking more than one brother is here.

"You ready to dance, Seda?"

"Why, yes I am, Layern, even with Palmer."

"Ok, your choice," I say. Getting out of the car to open her door, my eyes scan her body in seconds. She's wearing a red backless dress jumper. Her words not mine, it's very nice, and those heels, she can keep them on in bed tonight.

We walk into the bar holding hands, and I spot my brothers instantly, Gemi, Domlen, Hawken and crazy Warton. Seda spots them too, turning to me she whispers.

"Please."

"I promise nothing will happen if you don't dance with him, you can speak with him, but dancing, it's not going to happen. You are welcome to dance with my brothers, though."

"I'm an adult, in fact I'm three hundred and ten years old. I can dance with whom I please."

My brothers already have a table for us. We arrive and they all stand. She's met everyone but Hawken. He doesn't waste time introducing himself.

"Hello, Reseda. I'm Hawken, but you can call me Hawk."

"I think I'll call you Hawken, if you don't mind. Nice to meet you, too. I do have to ask, are you here to help your brother look foolish?"

"He doesn't need help in that department, but I'm here to make sure we stay secret among humans." He whispers the last word.

She glares at me as I pull out a seat for her. My brothers have drinks and bottles at the table. I pour some wine for myself and Seda. My brothers are talking to one another, but aware of the reason they are here.

"Reseda, what have you done to cause my brother to need us?" Gemi asks.

"I've done nothing. Your brother thinks he can control me. That will never happen," she responds.

My brothers and I go into hysterics with laughter. If Seda thinks she's going to win this battle against me, she's wrong. I plan on dancing with her, and I may let Gemi dance with her. Warton and Hawken, they are off limits. The music is loud, just the way I like. The bass is just right. I stand, holding my hand for Seda to dance. She can't help but say yes. Her body is moving as we head to the dance floor. We stroll to the middle of the dance floor, and as I let go of her hand she starts with a quick dip to the floor, coming up slow up against my body. My legs start to move, Seda's head is looking down, I reach out and lift her head, and our eyes meet. Smiling, I place a hand on her hips, moving my body against hers in a wave motion. Our dance gets attention. Other dancers move off the floor, giving us room, and she turns her back to me and we begin to step together, while her arms are lifted above her head. I glance at my brothers, only to find Hawken and Gemi are looking at Seda in a new light. I smile, knowing she's all mine. I continue dancing with my lecena, grinding against her, swirling my hips against her ass before I decide to turn her to face me. She's such a great dancer. She lifts a leg, bringing it up and down in a seductive move. The beat is just my style. I dip low, catching her leg, licking her ankle. Her body twists like a snake. It's beautiful to see her move so smoothly. I don't care about the crowd. I move to the floor, grabbing her waist as she moves, and my body is in sync with hers. She pushes and gives me a show, grinding in front of me, swaying her hips. I stand, giving her a show as well, my legs begin to stomp as I move grinding towards her, and step back as she moves towards me. She smiles, liking the chase, my lecena is so damn sexy.

I'm really getting into the dance as Palmer walks in. Seda's eyes are closed and I'm thankful they are. I speak to my brothers in my head, informing them the guy is here. They all look in his direction. His eyes are all over my lecena, lusting after her body. I smile as Warton comes and stands by him. I use my super hearing advantage, tuning into their conversation.

"She's pretty," Warton says.

Palmer glances over and has to look up, Warton stands at six foot seven.

"That's my best friend, and she's gorgeous." He smiles at her.

"She looks taken."

"Why the fuck are you talking to me?"

"Touchy, but I will let that slide. I'm the brother of the guy she's dancing with, and she's not available."

"Get the fuck away from me," Palmer yells. "You and this Layern guy are full of shit. I'm not intimidated by you."

Warton smirks.

"The next time you speak to me in that tone, I'm going to slam your face into that wall. Now, go seek another female. That one is taken."

"Another female, what age are you from? I'm Reseda's friend, not yours, and don't threaten me."

"Why?"

"I brought backup, too." He smiles.

In walks a very sexy woman with long, beautiful hair, but she's dangerous. She has all my brothers' attention. Gemi is out of his seat, but she stops him with a hand gesture. I smile, feeling Gemi is intrigued with this strange woman.

"Well, unless it's my father, I'm the scariest thing in here," he says, emphasising the word 'thing'.

"We will see."

Seda opens her eyes and spots Palmer and Warton exchanging

words. She turns, narrowing her eyes at me, and with a shrug I smile, and tune them out to listen to her.

"Layern, please don't let your brothers cause a scene or hurt my friend."

"Seda, no one will get hurt if he doesn't try to dance with you."

She starts walking through the dancing crowd towards Palmer, and I walk behind her, my eyes shooting daggers at him. Finally reaching him, she gives him an apologetic smile. I don't give him anything but a glare. I notice the woman standing next to him glares at me. Who the fuck is this female? She's got balls of steel, though.

"Palmer, I'm so glad you came." Reseda gleams.

"Yeah, sorry I'm late. I'd like to introduce my cousin, Shalisi." He waves to her.

"Hi, Reseda. Palmer has told me so much about you. It's very nice to meet you, finally." Seda and I are both shocked.

"Nice to meet you, I... I'm sorry, Palmer has never told me about you, ever," Reseda says, hurt.

I'm trying to pick up something on this female, Shalisi, but I can't get anything, in fact if she were not standing in front of me I would not even feel her at all. That's very strange, so I put my arm around Seda's waist for protection, and to show possession of her.

My brothers are all around now, Hawken is standing behind Palmer. Gemi is behind Shalisi, staring her up and down. He's really feeling her, and Warton is at Palmer's side, arms swinging loosely, ready for anything.

"I just came to town for Palmer. I'm usually a loner, but he's being bullied." Shalisi glares at me. She doesn't look at my brothers. I give her a nod and I still can't pick anything up on her. She's alive; I can hear her heart beating, smell her warm blood, but after that, empty.

"Well, Reseda, I would like a dance. Our song is playing," Palmer says, rubbing his hands together. It's 'Climax' by Usher. He and my lecena are not dancing, and definitely not dancing to a song called Climax. I make her climax.

"Palmer, Seda is not dancing with you," I snap.

He looks at her and then at me.

"Reseda makes her own decisions. She wants to dance with me, and you're not stopping it," he yells.

That's when his help, Shalisi, speaks.

"Now, Layern, you and your brothers don't want to cause problems. I mean you guys do have a secret to protect."

All at once our eyes are on her, and she has a wicked grin plastered on her face. Who the fuck is this bitch? Reseda looks at her strangely too. Gemi is the only one admiring this suicidal female.

"It would be wise of you not to piss me or my brothers off. I am, however, very concerned that you speak of me in such a manner. It seems you know of us, but we know nothing about you." I step closer, invading her space. Seda steps with me, holding my arm. As if she could hold me. Warton is in full beast mode.

"Wait, wait, please, I don't want this. Palmer, I can't dance with you, not today," Reseda says.

"Not ever!" I glare.

"Reseda, if you want to dance with Palmer, I can hold off the bullies," Shalisi says, smiling.

I never wanted to rip a woman's head off before now.

"I'm getting ready to go. Nice meeting you, Shalisi, but if you came here thinking I'm a victim, you are wrong. I choose to keep the peace. Layern, please take me home," Reseda says.

Palmer looks ashamed. She quickly kisses his cheek before I snatch her back. Seda pulls away from me, walking out of the bar. If she's pissed, I'm on fucking fire right now. I turn, but not before I speak.

"I'm taking my lecena home. Palmer, you and I will speak, and as for you, female, you just went up on a list you should never have wanted to be on."

"I like being number one," Shalisi smiles.

I walk away, leaving my brothers. I know they will leave soon. I sense Gemi is aroused by this woman. She's very beautiful, I have to admit, but she knows us, and now that's another mystery to uncover. FUCK!

RESEDA

I can't believe this shit! I was having a normal, well, semi-normal life, but I had to see Layern in Noke. Now he's living with me. His brothers show up whenever they like and my best friend Palmer's life could be in danger. Why does the sex have to be so damn good? I walk through my door, still not speaking. I can't believe what just happened, and who is this woman? She's way too pretty. Palmer has never mentioned this cousin. He must be lying. I storm upstairs, feeling Layern's presence behind me, but I will not acknowledge him. All this because of a dance. This is unacceptable.

After taking off my clothes, I walk into the shower, ignoring Layern's eyes on me. He hasn't said one word since we left the bar. I know this Shalisi girl has him upset. Hell, I'm upset. How did she know they were his brothers? Palmer could have told her, but knowing his family, that's strange. I welcome the hot water, closing my eyes and letting the water run over my hair. Then I feel arms around my waist.

"Layern, please, this is not the time."

"It's always the time. You angry with me?"

"I'm angry about this entire situation." I turn and face him. "Layern, why are you really here?"

"I told you."

"No you told me something, but I feel like you are hiding more. Your mother hates me, yet your brothers show up at my house, at the bar. Queen Nala would not allow this."

I watch to see if I can see anything that will tell me the truth, but nothing shows on his face. He doesn't speak, pulling me close to him. With his eyes on me, he slowly comes down to my mouth. Though I should stop him, my body doesn't push away, and I find my hands in his hair as our lips touch. He's gentle with this kiss, and everything south aches for his touch. I moan "Mmmm," and his tongue is in my mouth. He holds me captive. I couldn't get away even if I wanted to. Layern takes a step forward and pushes me backwards until I'm against the wall. I guess this is his way of saying he's really here for me. I'm not sure, but right now I need him and he obviously needs me. His hands and my hands are touching each other all over our bodies. Nothing is off limits. Once he enters me, I'm in a bliss that's so amazing. It's like the best dream of sex with a man, only it's not a dream. I'm really having sex with Layern, in my shower again. I close my eyes and enjoy my need, while fulfilling his.

***

Layern's body is wrapped around me. I smile, loving the feeling I get when I'm near him. He looks peaceful when he sleeps. I feel him tighten as I move. I sigh, wishing I could get up and just think.

"Relax," he says, eyes still closed.

"I want to get up."

"No."

Layern can be so trying sometimes.

"Layern, I'm hungry."

"Lie."

Fuck, I had forgotten he can tell with his gift. I was able to block him, but now I can't seem to block him at all.

"That's because you feel something for me."

"Layern, stay out of my feelings, please."

"Stay in bed, I like your naked body against me."

I smile hearing those words, enjoying them more than I should. He hasn't responded to my questions. I glance at the clock on the wall and it's after four in the morning, I wonder if he's up to talking. He responds with a twist of his body, and I feel his erection pressing against my back. I guess talking is out of the question again, but in the morning I will get answers.

***

The smell of bacon wakes me. I turn to touch Layern, but he's not in the bed. I sit up, and my body commands me to lie down. Layern is insatiable, but I wouldn't change a thing. I hear the door open, and I'm greeted by a naked Layern with a tray of breakfast. I did want bacon, but seeing him smiling at me with food, maybe food can wait.

"No, food is a must, Lecena, besides, you are extremely sore, don't try to stand." He chuckles.

"Well, if I can't have you for breakfast, stop standing there looking edible and bring the food over here, please." I smile.

"Edible, huh?"

"Yes."

He walks over on the other side of the bed, climbing in with the tray. It looks so good, he's cooked two pounds of bacon at least, a dozen or more eggs, and toasted a whole loaf of bread. He holds up one hand with a jar of strawberry jam and a gallon of milk. I didn't see the milk before, his body is very distracting. I smile to myself.

"Seda, you should eat, before I forget how sore you are. I'll give you a bath and then I will answer your questions."

Wow! Didn't expect that, but I'm glad he is going to come clean. I need the truth about why he's here. I take a piece of bacon, eating it slowly. Do I really want to know? This may change my feelings, and all this happiness I'm feeling now will end. We eat everything he's cooked. He doesn't speak, as usual. I wonder why no talking?

"We never talk while we eat on Earth, it's not our home," he simply says.

He rises, walking into the bathroom, and I hear the water running. My nerves are in my stomach; soon this feeling of being wanted could be over. He returns, picking me up and entering the bathroom, the water is sparkling with the prettiest blue ever, and I didn't know water could sparkle. Layern is looking at me, and I look into his eyes, feeling more than just a *like* feeling. He sits still with me in his arms, and begins to wash me, and with every touch, soreness leaves my body. Tears fill my eyes, it feels like this could be the end of us. He doesn't speak, just continues to wash me, and press soft kisses on my lips, cheeks, and shoulders.

When we have finished bathing, we climb out and he puts on some loose, light blue slacks. They look like something he would wear in Cortamagen. I slip on a dress, not bothering with underwear. We sit in the library, on the sofa, staring at one another. I swallow, waiting for the blow.

"I first have to say, I'm here because I want to be, and I really like you very much." Layern looks away for a second, then back at me. "You are right, I'm not here just for that reason. I'm telling you something that could get me severely punished by Queen Nala, but I can't be here without you knowing the truth."

I get up and start pacing around, my emotions getting out of control. My father used to tell me to keep them under control, I usually get out of control. Layern is at my side stopping me.

"Breathe," he commands. Oh shit, I was holding my breath.

"What I feel for you, it's real."

"I can't wait for this, just fucking tell me!" My emotions are out of control now.

"Queen Nala said that if I must see you again it had to be with the purpose of finding out what you know."

"WHAT?"

"Please, just listen, I never intended to tell her anything, I said I would keep you safe, and my promise is real. I don't even really know what she wants to know."

I feel disgusted. He was only sleeping with me to gain information. My body is moving strangely, and it feels like fire right now.

"Seda, you need to take deep breaths. Your beast wants out. I know you think I used you, but please look into my eyes. I never used you. I swear on my life."

"Fuck you!" I say. The voice that leaves me is unfamiliar, it's not me. What's happening? Layern tackles me to the ground.

"Listen, you can't change in the house, Seda. Close your eyes, please! I don't want to put you to sleep by force."

I've never changed before, and though I'm mad as hell at him, he's right. I close my eyes tight, and I feel him blowing on me, and my body begins to relax. It's a strange feeling. It feels good, almost sexual. I still can't speak, he's here to spy on me. I open my eyes and close them again and he starts that blowing again, grinding his body on mine, a sexual need is there.

"STOP!" I scream.

Layern doesn't listen, but continues his movements, and soon my body is moving with him. I feel his arousal through his slacks, they are very thin, and my dress doesn't have much material. He presses and I moan, "Ahhhh!" I don't want this, but I need it. Stopping is my only option, and finally I find a voice to speak.

"I'm calm, please get off me."

"I'm sorry, Seda."

"Just get up NOW!"

"Ok."

We both get off the floor, and I glare at him.

"Seda, we need to talk."

"Talk, you want to talk now, I don't know anything, and if I did I'm taking it to my grave."

"I don't care about my mother or why you are banned, I just care about you, Seda. Please don't be angry. You are very angry right now."

"Layern, you have been sleeping with me to get information."

"What information have I got? Think about it, Seda. I was bedding you because I enjoy you."

"Well, it's over. No more enjoyment from me."

"I'm not letting you go."

"Leave my house."

He starts walking towards me and I sprint around the couch. I'm not letting him touch me. It will end with him being inside me. He tries again to come towards me, and I run again. Now he's behind the sofa and I'm in front of it.

"I will tackle you, Seda. Don't run, and I'm not leaving you."

"I'm not talking, so you should go. I'll take whatever, and the promise Queen Nala has for me."

"I've hidden your mother already, Seda. Please, just sit. I promise to keep my hands to myself."

Glaring at him, I walk slowly around to the sofa and take a seat. This is all my fault, I should never have let Layern get so close. Now my life, and my mother's life, will end.

"Why? Is your mother searching for her?"

"No, she's not. I did it to prove to you I'm on your side, but for me to help you I need leverage."

"Leverage? I thought you said she's not in trouble. You need to take me to my mother."

He pauses, taking a deep breath.

"Why did my mother ban you from Kalin?"

"You should ask her," I snap.

He looks at me and those blue eyes are soft and filled with concern, but he fooled me. I should have known something was up, why would a prince want me? We are both silent, and he starts walking towards me and I don't move, he comes so close without touching, but his body is an inch from mine. If I move we will touch. Layern closes his eyes and speaks.

"I'm asking you. My mother, Queen Nala, will not be honest, but you will." His words are like fire. His breath smells good, and the heat from him is consuming me.

"I have no information, Prince Layern," I say. I was merely

another he could add to the list of many.

"Layern, Lecena. It's Layern, not Prince."

"Well, though I've been banned from Kalin, I know the rules of the Draglen brothers, and I will not disrespect you. I hope you found much pleasure with me," I say, calmly. I could breathe fire at this moment.

"Please stop with the sarcasm." He sighs. "Listen, I never tried to get information from you, but I'm asking now. I'm trying to lift the ban from you, Seda. I want you to come to Cortamagen, see my home. Don't you want to see your mother all the time?"

He thinks he can help me.

"You can't help me, so just stop."

"Yes, I can."

"No, just leave, Layern. Why are you making this difficult? You got what you wanted."

"Excuse me? You think I just wanted to bed you, fuck you, and make love to you? All for information? You think nothing of me." He glares. Anger is rolling off him and crowding my space. I step back and he steps forward.

I'm not going to feel sorry for what I said. This is his fault, not mine. He came here for information for his mother. Queen Nala wants me dead. Why does she want information? What does she think I know? Maybe Layern is right. She doesn't want me to tell something that could be damaging. What's more damaging than banning the daughter of the man you wanted? Oh, that's it! Queen Nala never told anyone about my father, the man she and my mother both loved.

"Layern, please step back, I don't want to be around you right now."

He pauses for a minute, and then he steps to the side. I take this space and walk out the door, and head for my father's grave. I really need him now. Layern doesn't follow that I can see, but I'm sure he will be waiting for me when I get home. I cry all the way to my father's tombstone. When I finally get there, I just sit in front of it, rubbing his name. Queen Nala hates me because of my existence. I'm caught in a love triangle that has caused me to be punished. I begin to speak to my father the only way I can, now.

"Dad, why did you have to die? I need you right now. I broke a promise. I kept seeing that Prince Layern," I say, as tears begin to fall. "He was here on orders, Dad, from Queen Nala. He says he wanted to be here with me, but can I believe that? He says he wants to help me, Dad. You were all the help I ever needed, but you're gone now. I don't like being by myself and that's how I feel, by myself. I would trade or do anything for just another minute with you. Please, Dad, give me a sign. I don't know what to do."

"You are not alone, Seda, and I want to help you," Layern says. I turn and he's standing behind me. Could he really care?

LAYERN

I can't believe how much I have hurt her. I knew this was a bad idea, Queen Nala did this on purpose. Ruining my chance with Reseda. I followed her to know where she goes when hurt, and it's to a graveyard. A place for the dead, not the living. I listen to her speech to a grave, and my heart breaks for her. My lecena should not feel alone. She starts crying when I tell her she's not alone. I drop to my knees, hugging her.

"Please, let me be there for you, Seda. I didn't want to hurt you. I was forced to do this, to seek information." I take a deep breath of her scent. "I was coming back to see you, but my mother said if I didn't get information she would personally come to Earth to kill you. I couldn't let that happen. I only said 'yes' to buy myself time to figure a way to get you out of this situation. That's the truth."

She doesn't respond, only sobbing into my chest. The only

thought for me is to wrap my arms around her. I know my time on Earth is coming close to an end. I have to go back, but I want Seda with me. If I leave, it only proves that she's alone, and she's not. I love her feistiness, her beautiful dancing, how she's independent, and she makes me forget everything but her. She finally pulls back and looks up at me, her face red from all the crying.

"Can you take me home, please?" she asks, through dry sobs.

"Yes, I will take you home."

We make it home in no time, and my only concern is to get her into bed to rest. It's still early in the day, but she almost changed into a dragon on me. That can take your strength. She needs to sleep while I think of a plan. I won't let her be alone any more. Seda falls asleep fast, and I stay with her until I'm sure she's in a deep sleep.

***

Seda's library is filled with books from Kalin, and I go in search of some way to keep her safe from my mother. I search and search for a clause that releases a ruling of the throne. There's nothing for a long time and then I stumble upon one. It's not my first choice, but I will do it to keep her alive and safe. I'm just not sure how she will take it, or how I can get this done? I don't think I can tell anyone this. It's a huge risk, and it's going to be dangerous for me as well. I take a deep breath and get on the phone, setting up what will be a life-changing event for me.

The hours slip by me, and when I look up, it's late afternoon. Seda is still sleeping, but I will make something to eat and get her up. We have a couple of days to get this squared away.

As I walk into the kitchen deciding what to make, my Cortamagen phone rings. It's Showken.

"Brother, when are you coming home?"

"Soon, how's the Young coming?"

"Oh, he's coming along fine, Marilyn is ready for him to come. I don't have the heart to tell her another four weeks, I think the breathing fire and not sleeping is getting to her."

"Brother, I can't wait to hold your Young," I say.

I need the conversation to stay off me. I know he has called to grill me about Seda, but right now is not the time.

"Ok. I can't either. Now, on to more pressing business, when do I get to see this red-haired female?"

"Showken, you can't come to Earth, and she's not allowed in Kalin."

"I know that, send a fucking picture. Draken and I both want to know who has gotten you after all these years. So, is she good in bed?"

"Showken, is Marilyn good in bed?" I ask.

I know he's not going to like it back.

"My Wella should not be discussed about how fabulous she is in bed, this half-breed is not your Wella, so tell me, brother."

"It's a secret, talk to you soon, brother."

"How soon?"

"Shit, Showken, where is Marilyn, you are full of questions."

"Well, whatever you're doing, hurry. Queen Nala is in a foul mood, and between her and Mari, I've been painting while I can."

I don't want to rush him, but I need to get Seda up.

"I'm taking care of it, brother, give my love to Marilyn."

"I will."

The phone goes dead and I quickly make some steaks, raw vegetables, and mashed potatoes. I'm a little nervous about telling Seda my plan. She's going to think I'm crazy, but really, it's her only choice. I set up the tray with food and heading up stairs, I find my lovely lecena sleeping. I've never been afraid to say anything, but I'm about to tell Seda her only option, she might choose death.

"Lecena, wake up, my lecena," I whisper in her ear. Her body stirs seductively, and I look down to see I'm fully erect and ready. This is not the time, later though, the cover slips and her nipples are hard, shit! Definitely later.

"Wake up, Seda, I've got food for you." She gives a slight smile, dragons can't resist food. Her eye creaks open, and closes quickly. What's she doing?

"Oh, how long have I been asleep?"

"You needed rest, Seda. Don't worry about how long. Now, let's eat."

We both dive in and eat, smiling at each other between bites. It's nice to see her smiling. I will try to keep her from crying again. My heart can't stand to see her tears. She's truly a precious lecena. She's doesn't deserve the ban that has been placed on her. Seda is a dragon too, and my mother will have to accept her back into Kalin.

"Layern, I see you didn't listen when I asked you to leave."

"No, I told you I wasn't going to leave, but I did a lot of research while you were sleeping."

She looks at me suspiciously, but holding up my hands, I smile, hoping to get her to relax.

"What were you researching? Me?"

"No, I was researching how to lift the ban, and I've found a way."

"There's no way to lift the ban. Your mother would have to do that, and Layern, she's not going to lift the ban."

"She will have to, if my plan works."

"What are you up to?"

Here goes, please let her agree to this. I don't have any other idea.

"Reseda Fire, will you marry me?"

The silence in the room is unnerving. She looks speechless. I try to get a read, but I come up blank. Damn, she's blocked me again.

"No, no, no, no, no... no."

Well damn, she's hurt my pride. That's a lot of no's she's said. I have to make her understand the reasoning behind this.

"Look, in my research, if the King or Queen bans a person from Kalin, they may return without fear of harm for themselves or their family if they marry, or what we call conete, to a descendant

143

of the King or the Queen. It's your lucky day. I just happen to be a Draglen Brother."

She climbs out of bed, naked, and I can't hear her talking. Her afla is very distracting. I finally tune back in, only to hear her say, "I don't want to get married."

"Why? You will be fully taken care of and we are great in bed, and you can come to your real home and see your mother."

"Layern, you don't just marry someone because of that, I'm not marrying you to get unbanned."

"It's the only option we have. I've searched through everything, and, Seda, it won't be so bad. After five years we can part, and then you will be free from running and being separate from your mother."

"This plan is not going to work. She's going to kill me, and you will be punished beyond belief. Besides, they would not honor a marriage performed on Earth."

"Yes, they will honor it. I even checked into that. As long as we get married on any planet, we are good. I booked us a flight to Vegas."

"Layern, your mother will kill me, very slowly, for marrying her son."

"I'll worry about my mother. I just need you to say yes."

She starts pacing, and her breasts are doing a bounce. Wow, and that will be mine for five years. I'm going to bite her nipples hard. She finally stops in front of me and, taking a deep breath, I smell her sweet comfort zone.

"Layern, you are a nasty man."

"That's true. Will you marry this nasty man for at least five years?"

"You sure that they will have to honor this marriage, and we can get out of it in five years?"

"Yes, I'm sure, but we need to leave tonight, time is running out, my brother's Wella is with Young and I have to be there."

"Wait, I'm not going to Cortamagen, Layern. Your mother would kill me for sure."

"Trust me, now you need to get dressed, we can buy clothes when we get there."

"Wait, Layern, this is moving so fast! Married, really?

"Yes, really. Come on, let's go."

"Why do we have to go to Vegas, though?"

I smile. That's just something I've seen in human movies and always wanted to try.

"It will be fine, Seda. You are about to become my Wella."

I growl, knowing that I'll be able to keep her safe.

"How much time do I have?"

"Two hours, and then we catch my private jet to Vegas."

I will be in Cortamagen by morning, with a Wella. This will upset the family, but I'm not leaving Seda unprotected from my mother. She has left me no choice.

***

The plane ride gives me quality time with my lecena. Reseda and I spend most of the time in bed, with me loving her. We laugh and talk about her childhood, and how she and her father were so close. I find out Seda has degrees in medicine, physics, and linguistics. I enjoy getting to know more about her. I share with her about my brothers and how we can't be killed. She tells me she knows that, but I just want to remind her. I can't wait until she can come home with me.

We are met at the airport by a limousine. It's early October and the weather is alright, I like very hot weather.

"Layern, I need to shower and get a dress."

"Why?"

"If I'm getting married to you," she glares, "even if it's temporary, I want to have on a dress."

"Ok, we can stop at the hotel."

"Thank you… thanks for everything, Layern, you are special," she says, leaning over and giving me a soft kiss on the cheek.

"Any time, Lecena, any time."

Reseda finds a dress in the hotel, and spends a great deal of time getting ready. We finally get back into the car to go and say our vows. That's when I start getting nervous. I know this has to be honored, but I haven't told Seda that I will be subject to punishment.

"Layern, you ok?"

"Yes, I'm just thinking about getting you out of that dress. It's taking all my might not to let my erection show." I smile, and she blushes. She looks stunning in an off-white dress, it's halter style and very elegant, nothing over the top.

"Well, please keep that under control. That piece of you is dangerous."

"Yes, but it's all for you."

"For at least five years."

We finally get to a little chapel. It's small, extremely small, but it will do. Seda and I walk in hand in hand. She's nervous, but so am I. I never thought that when I took a Wella, it would be without my family. Yet here I stand alone with Seda, and I'm more than happy.

RESEDA

It went by so fast. I'm married to Prince Layern Draglen, holy shit! There are no words to describe this feeling. My only regret is that I wish my father and mother could have been here. I know it's a marriage of convenience, but I still feel like a real bride who's in love. Layern has done all this for me to keep me. I owe him everything. If I'm able to come to Kalin without fear and see my mother, it will be the best day of my life. We make it to our suite and it's beautiful. There are all sorts of flowers everywhere, roses, lilies, and even morning glories. It smells so great. There's a buffet of food and wine. I turn and see him smiling.

"All this for your temporary bride?"

"Why yes, now if you don't mind, I need to get you out of that dress."

Layern strolls towards me, undoing his tie, not looking away from my eyes.

"Your eyes are so beautiful. Can you keep them open when I make you come?"

My breath catches in my throat. We've done all sorts of things together, but he's my husband now. I nod without saying a word.

"Do you need food?" I ask.

"No, I need you. We have all night, because when the sun rises, we will go to Cortamagen."

He stops a few feet away from me and with his finger he gestures for me to turn around in a circle. Layern has never done this before, but I just do it. I'm his wife now. *Oh wow*! He comes closer and his shirt is open now. Swiftly, he picks me up and carries me into the bedroom. There are more flowers in here.

"Lecena, do you like your flowers?"

"Yes, they're gorgeous, thank you."

"I have more for you when we get home."

My dress is off before I can blink, and underneath I have deliberately worn some lingerie for him. A deep growl comes from him, which sends my body into need. He quickly removes my bra and with his teeth begins to pull down my lace panties. "Mmmm."

"Yes, Seda, I want to hear you very loud and clear, my name should leave your lips a thousand times, screaming in pleasure."

We freefall onto the bed, with him landing on top of me. He's not heavy, because I assume he's keeping most of his weight on his arms and legs. I'm totally naked now, and he is still in a shirt and pants. Smiling at him, I point to his clothes.

"Rip them off, love, there's no one here but you and me,

besides, I want your beast to get real comfortable with me."

I try not to use my strength, my father always said it would be dangerous, but I'm with a dragon. Shouldn't be any harm. I take hold of Layern's shirt and with one pull, I have it off his body and have ripped it from the sleeve still on his right arm. I push my hands into his pants, and he's not wearing any underwear. Licking my lips, I rip off the pants, and his erection is hard and ready. I want him in my mouth. Getting onto my knees on the bed, I lean over, taking him in my mouth, sucking and licking him. His hand glides over my butt in a circular motion. He coaxes my legs apart so he can have access to my sex as I get him off. Two fingers slip inside, filling the ache in me, pleasing him is my pleasure. Hearing his moans excites me. I can't stop sucking. He's huge, but I relax, taking him all in. I need this and I want this. Layern, using the wetness from my sex, lubricates my ass, and slips in his index finger. It's foreign, painful, but oh, feels so good. I think five years with him will not be bad at all.

He flips me onto my hands and knees, placing himself behind me, I feel him slapping his sex against my ass and I want him inside.

"LAYERN!" I yell.

"That's one, baby."

Did he really mean a thousand times? I'm in fucking trouble.

He's inside my sex fast, thrusting until I feel a building in my body and I scream again.

"LAYERN!"

"Two, Lecena."

Shit, he's counting.

He pulls out fast, and without warning, he bends over and pinches my nipple extremely hard and I scream, because he pushes inside my ass now. He doesn't move, the only sound is him and me both panting, soon he moves a little and it hurts like hell. He stops again, and moves a little more, this goes on for about five minutes, and eventually I push back for more.

"You want it?" he says.

"YES!"

The need is there, and very slowly he pulls out and slams back in, and I think I move forward. I'm not sure if he did that or if I was trying to get away. The building is coming again and I want this. So I push back, and this time he starts a rhythm with me. His fingers are pulling my nipples and his lips are on my back as he takes my entire body, making it his completely. I didn't know I could orgasm like this, but sure enough, I'm screaming his name and he's growling mine. We fall on the bed and I think he's done, but no - I'm flipped back over on to my back, and he starts on my front, licking, sucking, and biting, leaving no place untouched.

"You are mine, Seda."

"Yes."

We make love the entire night, breaking only for food, not even a shower is worth a break.

***

The morning comes too quickly. We have both showered, eaten and are ready to portal to Cortamagen.

"You ready?"

"No," I say honestly. This could be my last breath. Queen Nala will be waiting. Layern kisses my hand, and pulls out his portal.

"Let's go meet the family," he says.

We are off, and inside the portal I get a glimpse of his dragon as his face goes back and forth from the blue dragon to a blue-eyed man. It's amazing, I've never been in a portal with anyone else but myself. I close my eyes, and soon we are standing in a huge blue bedroom.

"This is where you will sleep, it's our room now, used to be just mine."

The realization hits me, I'm in Cortamagen with Layern, and I'm married. My head is spinning. Queen Nala is going to kill me. Layern wraps his arms around me, blowing a sweet scent over me, and soon I'm relaxed, until the door bursts open.

"Our mother wants you, brother, and bring her," Hawken says.

"She's my Wella, brother, don't disrespect me."

"You disrespect this castle by doing this."

Layern growls and before Hawken can move Layern shoots fire at him, hitting him in the chest. He pulls me close, and we walk past an angry Hawken holding his burned chest. The halls are so big and beautiful. The stones outside his room are filled with blue jewels. The Draglen Brothers are known for their wealth, among other things. I don't have time really to capture the beauty, because Queen Nala is waiting for us. We go through some doors that are big enough to fit a dragon, and enter a huge garden with a platform, a throne. The seating of his family is clear and everyone looks like royalty. Layern and I walk up the steps before Queen Nala stands. I see his other brothers and King Dramen on the throne next to her. I even see the only sister, Beauka, I'm not sure who the other women are. I'm assuming they are the Wellas of Draken and Showken.

"She's not allowed on these steps," Queen Nala snaps.

"If you want to speak with me, she's my Wella now. She comes and stays with me."

Layern and his mother are staring at each other and I know there is talking going on in their heads, because she lets out a yell.

She walks slowly down the steps and the brothers and the King rise, following her down. She stops one step away from us.

"I will forgive you, son, if you turn her over to me. You are not really married. It didn't happen here, and she's not taken you on."

"I love you, Mother, and I respect the Queen in you, but this is one thing on which I will not obey you. If you try to hurt Reseda, my Wella, you must kill me too."

I swallow hard as her eyes find me. I can feel her anger rolling over me. My body stiffens and Layern grips my hand harder. He steps in front of me, pushing me behind him. I frown. I'm not afraid of her. I have been waiting to confront her my entire life. I've been in a prison because of her, always fearing for my life and my mother's.

"My son, you speak of this woman as if you love her, but you married her only to defy me. I will move you out of the way if need be, but I want to see this brave soul willing to stand before me." Queen Nala speaks with authority.

"She's my Wella, speak to me."

I can't let him do this for me, pulling away from him I stand beside him, my head lifted and my shoulders back. I will not fear this evil witch, and if death comes, I'll welcome it after I say my piece.

"Have something to say?" Queen Nala asks.

I look at Layern and he shakes his head 'no' at me. I give him a smile.

"As a matter of fact I do, you evil witch," I growl. "Your son married me to keep you away from me and my mother. If I die, I die, but does everyone here know why you banned me, including King Dramen?"

I don't see it coming, but her hand hits me so hard that I fly through the air. I feel the pain before I hit the ground. I'm a good three hundred yards away, my head hits the ground and I feel the blood running from my mouth and my head. I hear Layern yell and I see him go for his mother, and with one hand she has him in the air, his feet off the ground. My eyes are wide and fearful, would she kill her own son? I take off in a sprint back to him. I stop to hear her speak.

"My son," she spits. "Come against me, based on a lie from an outcast. You will know my wrath, Layern." The brothers are all around, watching their brother struggle against her hand. I scream for help.

"PLEASE HELP HIM!" I cry. Gemi looks at me, hurt in his eyes. Finally Draken steps forward.

"Release him," he says.

"Draken, my oldest, stay out of this, I won't kill him, but he will wish he was dead."

"RELEASE MY FUCKING BROTHER!" Oh my, his voice travels past me, into the city.

"HE'S MY SON, BACK DOWN!" Queen Nala yells back. I'm not sure what is going to happen, but her eyes are beast. I see King Dramen lay his hand on her arm. She sets Layern down, and he is gasping for air. I run towards him and I'm lifted up in the air, with a ring around my neck. I'm completely still, I know that if I move I'm dead. Layern looks up and I see his beast coming forth. Draken comes to stand before her.

"Queen Nala, you are queen through marriage. I carry the Draglen blood. I am heir to the throne and as your future king, I command you to release Layern's Wella, before it gets really nasty."

"You will make a great king someday, but today you're not king."

King Dramen reaches his hand into the air, releasing Queen

Nala's hold on me, and lifts me, setting me behind him. I feel so helpless.

"Warton, Brumen, and Gemi, take Layern's Wella to his room. Stay with her, guarding her with your lives, until I say otherwise." The words are so powerful.

I'm torn away, but not before I see Draken and Showken helping Layern off the ground.

"Please let me stay," I sob. "Please, I have to be with him."

Soon I'm back in Layern's room, and I crawl into his bed and begin to cry harder. This is all my fault, if I could have stuck to the rules Layern would never have seen me. Now he's being hurt by his own mother. I hear his brothers talking outside my door. Then I hear a man's voice yelling. It sounds like Draken. The walls are trembling, and fear washes over me. What's happening?

I curl up in the middle of the bed. I try to control myself, praying that Layern is ok. I belong here. There's lots of yelling, and then silence. The door opens and King Dramen is standing there.

"Come and walk with me, child." He holds out his hand and stumbling out of the bed I make my way to him. "You're safe, my Queen can get angry, as you can see." He smiles, and I see why his sons are so gorgeous.

"Layern?"

"He's being taken care of, I would like a word with you first."

"Yes, King Dramen."

"Oh you're family, just Father, ok?"

"Yes."

We walk and he begins to talk to me about the land, stopping to introduce me to staff, and even one of the pets. It's a yellow, green-eyed dog roaming around. We stop and he hands me a piece of fruit. I'm unfamiliar with it, but it tastes like strawberry mixed with blueberry. He continues the walk, and I meet the cooks, and more servants. Soon we are walking beside a river. It's beautiful, and I see mermaids waving as we walk by. King Dramen is very handsome, with long black hair with small strings of grey, but he looks like Draken. Yet all his sons have the same smile. What does he want to talk about? He walks to a table that could seat twenty, takes the seat at the end and waves for me to take a seat beside him.

"Well, you are one beautiful dragon, Reseda, please tell me what's going on."

I take a deep breath. I'm far away from everyone, would he harm me too? King Dramen is not to be underestimated. He's the King of the most powerful place in Kalin.

"I'm not sure what you mean."

"How do you know the Queen?"

I shake my head, holding it down. If I speak and tell him, I'm not sure what he will do.

"You are safe with me, speak."

"Queen Nala banned me from Kalin."

"Why?"

"I'm half-dragon, and um... please... I'm not sure I'm the

right person to tell you this."

"You are the only person I want to tell me, now speak freely."

I take a deep breath and speak.

"Queen Nala and my mother were best friends, but they both fell in love with my father, but he loved my mother and they had me and Queen Nala was angry and banned me from Kalin, and made my mother a servant in Noke." I can't believe all that has come out of my mouth so fast.

"Where is your mother?"

"I'm not sure. Layern said he put her somewhere safe."

"How long?"

"Excuse me?"

"How long were you banned?"

"Forever."

I'm not sure how he's able to keep so calm. I just told him his wife was cheating on him. I lower my head, not meeting his eyes.

"I see, you love my son?"

"Yes, I do." Those words come easily out of my mouth. I do love Layern, he's my husband and I want to see him. "Can I see him?"

"You will be permitted to see him tonight, but after that, for thirty days, you will be separated."

My mouth drops open, tears roll down my face.

"Why?"

"My son, though he has a right to protect you, went about this entire thing in the wrong way, marrying without his family. Thirty days is my decision, not the Queen's. During that time you can prepare for a real ceremony with my son, but this temporary idea I don't agree with, either you accept him forever, or you leave now, returning to Noke if you choose."

"What are you saying?"

"I will welcome you in the castle, but it has to be forever, or I will grant you pardon and you can live among your people as you should have done from the beginning."

He's giving me a way out of this temporary marriage, do I really want out? Layern only married me to keep me alive, but now I can stay in Kalin and see my mother all the time without fear. I'm not sure what to say.

"Can I speak with Layern first?"

"You will see him tonight, you may talk with him then, but when the sun rises, you will not see him again for thirty days."

"Thank you… thank you so much." I begin to cry.

"Oh no tears, you will see him soon, his brothers are calming him down. He went to fly."

"He's in dragon form?"

"Yes, would you like to see?"

I shake my head.

"I think I'll wait to see another time."

"Let's walk back to the castle and have something to eat."

"Yes, that sounds great."

I can live in Kalin, without any threats, and I don't have anyone on Earth but Palmer to consider going back to visit. Here I

can be myself, with no judgment. I wish I could tell Palmer life has
gotten better for me.

LAYERN

SEDA! I yell her name over and over in my head. I don't even know if she's ok. My father took her away, and I'm sure he made sure she was taken care of, but it's my job, not his. Queen Nala tried to hurt me, her own son. I'm flying with Draken and Domlen, Showken had to go take care of his Wella, something I should be doing. I've already been told I have tonight with her, but after that thirty days away from my Wella. This will surely make her want to get away from me. She didn't get a welcoming party, all because my mother wanted a man who didn't want her. I think we have circled Kalin twice, and I still have energy to burn. Domlen dips low, indicating we are stopping now. We are back in Cortamagen, on Beauka's cliff. It's very neat, and she even has a blanket laid out. My brothers and I transform into humans so we can speak. There are no wraps for us on this cliff. Luckily we are very comfortable here in Kalin, and wear as few clothes as possible while still maintaining respect.

"Where is Reseda?"

"Father went for a walk with her, but I'm sure they are back now. We did fly for over three hours," Domlen says, calmly.

"Our father took Reseda on a walk? Why?"

"It was more like a tour of what could be her home," Draken chimes in. He comes from around the bush with desserts. Beauka is going to kill us, but Draken found them. We eat, but refuse to drink her tea. Beauka tea is deadly, literally.

"It's her home, Draken."

"Yes, but father told her that, instead of the temporary arrangement you told him about, he decided to let her choose you, without a threat hanging over her."

I throw the tiny cake in my hand off the cliff. I should never have told him. She's going to choose living without fear. She has no reason to stay with me in the castle, with my mother who hates her.

"What are you afraid of, brother?" Domlen asks.

"I'm not afraid, just sure she will choose a life separate from me, rather than live in a castle with our crazy mother."

"Then that will be your fault," he says, and Draken nods in agreement. "If you have been bedding her right, though you have to separate for thirty days, she will be clawing for you by then. If not, move on, brother, she was not meant for you."

"Domlen, I'm excellent in bed, but thirty days separation, she will have too much time to think about leaving me."

"He said you can't see her, nor speak with her, and remember her dreams are always an option," Draken says, raising a brow.

Yes, dreams are an option. I didn't think Seda and I would be apart. Now she's even given the option to leave me. I guess it's a good thing. I look at the sky and it's nearly sunset. I can get to my room and have her all night before I'm banned from her for thirty days.

"How are they going to keep us apart for thirty days? Did Father say?"

Draken and Domlen look at each other and I instantly get the read, fuck! I have to live away from the castle for thirty days. I don't want to be locked in a room. This is for the best, then, but she will still need protection from my mother.

"Draken, Reseda will need protection."

"Oh, Father has decided to protect her himself. I think he feels sorry for her."

"Well, I can't ask for anything better than the King himself protecting her. When is Marilyn's Young due?"

"Four weeks. So even if she does stay, the celebration will have to wait. Showken and Marilyn have been planning for their Young," Draken responds.

My brothers and I transform back to dragon, and fly back to the castle. We are greeted by servants holding wraps for us. Cess is in the garden, smiling at me. I stop to say hello.

"It's good seeing you smile, you make my brother really happy. So now, give us an heir."

"We are trying, Layern."

She goes to give me a hug, but Draken is there, picking her up and holding her out of my reach. I shake my head at him. Cess is not allowed to touch anyone male, and whoever tries to touch her could lose a limb.

I run to my room, opening the door to find Seda in a short blue gown. It barely covers her afla. I close the door, lock it and stare at her. She walks fast towards me.

"Are you ok? I was so worried when your mother was choking you."

"I'm fine, Lecena, How is your head, and your mouth?"

"Your father gave me some cream and all the pain is gone, and I don't even have a scar on my lip."

"I'm sorry I couldn't stop her from hitting you."

I should have known Queen Nala would strike out. Seda shouldn't have had to take a hit like that, and she's half human.

"Layern, don't, I'm fine. We only have tonight, then we can't see each other for thirty days."

"Where did you get this gown? I like it." I wrap my arms around her, hoping she will choose me.

"A very pregnant lady and another stopped by and gave me this, along with some other goodies for tonight."

"Did they? Their names are Cess and Marilyn."

"I know their names, Layern. Now, are we going to talk, or can you please make love to me?"

I bend down and scoop her into my arms, and I'm rewarded

with laughter. She's happy with me. Perhaps she will choose me after all. I walk her to our bed and lay her down softly. She stretches out in front of me, and seeing her on my bed in Cortamagen gives me joy. Her red hair is perfect against my blue sheets. She's perfect! My hands slide up her legs, pushing them apart. No panties, she's learning. The sight is beautiful. Her body aches for me. Her sex glistens for me. She. Is. Mine. I bend down, taking a slow lick of her center. It's like tasting her for the first time. Her moans are loud and welcomed. Opening her folds I suck on her clitoris, bringing her almost there before pulling back. Tonight will be about slow, not fast. I need to remember as much of her as possible before my sentence begins.

"Layern, please, make me come."

She's not going to make it easy with the show I can see.

"Listen, you will not get any rest tonight, not even a break, ok?"

"I hope you make good on that promise. Thirty days without you is a long time."

I flip her over, pulling off her blue gown, and begin to massage her body. She's tense, and I let my hands ease her mind. Using my fingers and a little pressure, I work her shoulders, arms, back, ass, and thighs. After using my hands, my lips and tongue are a must. Placing a hand at the nape of her neck I kiss the side of her neck, and I feel her smiling. My Wella likes sex as much as I do. I bite her shoulder, and plant a kiss on it. I can smell her arousal increasing. I'm kissing her all over her back, leaving bite marks that will last thirty days. When I make it to her round ass, I squeeze both cheeks hard and give her a kiss on each one. She moans louder, then cries out.

"LAYERN!"

"That's four."

"I need you inside me now," she pleads.

I need her, too, but I haven't finished her massage yet. I move to her feet and put pressure on spots that give her more pleasure. She tries to turn over, but I place my hand on her lower back, keeping her still. I can't hold out, not being inside her. I pull her hips up so her ass is in the air, and very slowly I enter her sex. She's dripping wet, and her walls tighten around me. I'm still trying to hold out longer. I begin at a fast pace, reaching and pulling her hair to keep her in place as I fall into the most comfortable place ever.

"AHHH!"

"Lecena, you feel so good, baby."

"LAYERN!"

"Five, baby," I pant out. She's close and so am I.

I can't hold on any longer at this speed, she tightens and I feel and smell her juices dripping down my leg, and soon I follow her with my own orgasm. We both fall onto the bed, utterly spent.

"Round two, Seda, flip over. I want those beautiful legs on my shoulders."

"Anything for you."

I spend the rest of the night making love to Seda, never giving her a break, and we eventually get to ten, before she passes out from exhaustion.

***

It is ten minutes before I have to leave, so I wake her.

"Seda, baby, please wake up."

"Mmmm, Layern, I don't think I can go again."

"Me either, but it's almost time for me to go."

She turns into me, burying her face in my chest, and I lean down, smelling the intoxicating smell of her.

"Thirty days."

"Yes, but I will speak with you."

"Layern, please, don't get in more trouble."

"My father said I can't see you for thirty days. I will speak with you, don't worry, Lecena."

"Where will you be?"

"I have a spot where I can hang out for thirty days."

She looks at me jealously. This is going in the right direction.

"I have a Wella, and I wouldn't dare stay with a woman." I sigh. "I know the offer my father gave you, and I want you to know I want you, not temporarily, but forever."

"Layern, I…"

"You don't have to answer now, just think about it, ok?"

I lean down, giving her a passionate kiss, pouring my heart into her in just this kiss. I want her to choose me over everything.

"Layern, I wish you didn't have to go," she says, crying.

"No crying, I will contact you later tonight, or tomorrow. I'm sure my father will make sure I'm nowhere near the castle to see you."

I hear footsteps coming.

"Listen, I have to get up and go, but please think of me. My father is protecting you."

The knock on the door comes, and she wraps her arms around me.

"I wish you could stay, Layern."

I have to leave this room, before she has me in tears.

I climb out of the bed, and quickly pull on some loose navy slacks.

"Prince Layern, King Dramen says you must leave, sir."

"I'm coming," I yell at the door. Seda is in full-on tears now. I walk to the door to open it, and find two servants standing waiting for me.

"Stay away from my sister, stick with Cess," I say, as the door closes. I hear her scream my name. I walk down the hall and spot all my brothers, in blue slacks like me. They're honoring me. We have never been apart for punishment reasons before. This is a first. Draken, Showken, Gemi, Warton, Brumen, Domlen, Fewton and Hawken. I hear her before I see her.

"Layern, I wore a blue dress just for you. If you need anything, please let me know, and I will watch over your Wella," Beauka says, then without warning slams into me, hugging me tightly.

"Thanks, Beauka. I'll be back, and please don't scare Seda away."

I hug each of my brothers and walk out the gates leading into the forest. I turn and look at the castle, and that's when tears start flowing, when I look back at the only home I know. I walk far into the woods, to my hiding spot. I've built a small lodge and stocked it with food, and the lake is nearby for bathing. Thirty fucking days!

RESEDA

I've been banned from Kalin for three hundred and ten years, and now that I'm welcomed back, I'm banned from Layern for thirty days. I don't want to leave this bed. After crying until no more tears will come, and I'm reduced to dry sobs, I finally fall asleep. The knock at the door wakes me.

"Reseda, it's me, Cess. I'm coming in," she says. The door opens, and she walks in with a very pregnant Marilyn.

"Come on, get up and shower. Wait - did he fuck you all night?" Marilyn asks.

Wow, she's very forward, I see. Before I can answer, another lady, whom I've never met before, comes in. She's a human. I frown in confusion.

"Reseda, this is my best friend, Jasmine, but everyone calls her Jazz."

The woman just starts talking.

"That's some low down dirty shit the Queen done to you," Jazz says. "I'm on your side. I say every time you see her, flip her off."

"Wait, you never said if you can get up, can you?" Cess chimes in.

They are not letting up on that question. Of course, we had sex all night. Walking right now is going to be difficult.

"Yes, Layern kept me up all night."

"Really, spill the juicy details," Jazz says, smiling.

"Are you a Wella to one of the brothers?" I ask her. I like her, she's very down to earth. I will need this for thirty days.

"I'm not yet, but skippy is a punk if I don't wed someone in this land," Jazz laughs.

She's a pretty girl, short hair, green eyes and a body that doesn't stop, neither does her mouth.

"We can't ask a brother to put you in the bath, because Layern would fight them, maybe even burn them, but we could move you," Cess says, apologetically.

I'm in my bed, can't walk because Layern didn't go easy on me, and now I need women to help me into the tub.

"I can't lift a fly," Marilyn says with attitude. "Showken would feel that I'm doing something that I shouldn't and then he would be in here, and Reseda, I don't know you that well, you're under that sheet naked, you're not getting near my man."

I don't want Showken, I want Layern.

"I can help you, and Jazz can, too," Cess says. She's beautiful.

I move some, and moan in pain, feeling the soreness everywhere. They all smile as if they are remembering their own soreness.

"Come on, red dragon, we got to get you in the tub." Jazz and Cess come and place my arms under their shoulders, and quickly drag me to the bathroom. They sit me on the side of the tub, and I'm amazed at the beauty in here. There are jewels on the walls. The ladies are talking away, but start the water, and Cess pours something from a small glass bottle into the water. This is Layern's oil, and it makes me smile. He knew I would need it, and he's still looking after me, even though he's away.

"Red dragon?" I ask, smiling. Never heard that before.

"Yes you're a dragon, with red hair. Besides, 'red dragon' might scare the Queen."

"Nothing scares her."

"Oh, yes, she has her own fears, Reseda, you will see." Cess smiles.

I slip into the water, and the heat, along with Layern's oil, is the best. The ladies leave me for privacy, vowing to come back in one hour. I could sit in this water for an hour. These thirty days are to decide if I want out of my marriage with Layern. I really like him, in fact I love him, but I would get my freedom back, get to spend time with my mother. I haven't been able just to be free, ever. If I commit to Layern, that's some freedom gone. The ladies are not giving me much to think about. After about twenty minutes of relaxing, I wash, and climb out of the tub feeling amazing. My body is no longer sore, and I feel like walking around again.

Palmer crosses my mind as I walk back into the bedroom. I'm sure he's going crazy with worry, but dealing with him is just too much right now. He and I will talk soon. I'm hoping to see my mother, but Layern has hidden her, and I might have to wait until he comes home. The ladies brought me some dresses yesterday, with the gown, so I slip on a long blue dress. It touches the floor. Not my style, but I'll wear it. It fits my body perfectly. It's not long before there's a knock at the door, and I answer to see Gemi standing there, he sure is a sight to see. Those gentle grey eyes, his body is solid and he licks his perfect lips, I stop myself from looking at him any further.

"I'm here to escort you to the garden for some food and just chatting, we call it 'meech'.

I'm going to learn so much with this new freedom.

"Will it be ok? I mean, could I get hit again?"

"You are sitting next to the King, Reseda. My mother is brave, but not brave enough to cross King Dramen."

Oh, Cess did say she has her fears. Maybe King Dramen is one of them.

"Ok, let's go, then."

He holds his arm out for me. I tuck my hand into his elbow and we walk to the garden together. I miss Layern already.

"Gemi, I thought the ladies were coming back?"

"They were, I told them I would collect you and meet them at the meech."

"Why?"

He frowns, but doesn't stop walking, did I say something wrong?

"My brother would want me to make sure you were ok, this is my way of showing support to him."

"Layern is jealous, you know."

"My brother only shows jealousy where there is a need. Like with Palmer, but neither I nor my brothers would ever hurt him in such a way," he says, sternly.

We come to a set of beautiful, huge doors, draped in jewels and flowers, this place is beautiful, Noke is not as pretty as here.

Gemi looks over at me as I stand there in awe, smiling at how a place can be so marvelous. The wind blows and I catch a beautiful smell. It's one of the best smells ever. I mean, Layern's smell is the best. How can I eat with his family, with him not here? It seems wrong.

"Reseda," Gemi whispers to me, "you will have plenty of time to look around, but the family is waiting."

My eyes leave the beauty of the garden, and I look at Layern's family watching me. Swallowing hard, I begin to walk toward them. They are all sitting at a very long table, just waiting. Draken is looking at me without any expression, Warton narrows his eyes, and King Dramen has a small smile across his face. I'm uncomfortable already. This will be strange.

I come close and all the men stand, except the King. All eyes are on me, and out of fear I take a step back, but turn to see Gemi is right behind me shaking his head 'no'. I turn back and look at everyone, and King Dramen calls my name. I can't help but see and feel Queen Nala's eyes piercing me.

"Reseda, Wella of Layern, please come sit. You are safe." King Dramen smiles.

I see three empty seats between Showken and Warton. Gemi sits next to Warton, and I take a seat next to him. I realize that the third seat is for Layern. Instantly my eyes are searching to see if he will walk up. Gemi looks at me and shakes his head 'no', again. Fuck! All the men sit, and servants come from everywhere placing plates of food on the table. Everyone is eating and talking, it's like they are ignoring me, until I see Queen Nala's eyes are still glaring at me. She hates me and I hate her. Then I hear Marilyn.

"Showken, you don't have to feed me. I can do it myself." She giggles. Showken ignores her requests, continuing to feed her grapes and berries. She looks so beautiful. Cess speaks to me.

"Reseda, you look frightened, but I can tell you everyone at this table, including my love, is sweet. Enjoy, Layern would want you to."

"I'm not sure about that," I say, taking a bite of warm bread.

The table chatter starts to die down.

"If any one of my brothers does or says anything disrespectful," Cess says confidently, "I, Marilyn, Jazz and their baby sister Beauka will get them. None of them, not even the great warrior Warton, wants to mess with Beauka." All the women look at me and smile. I nod, accepting their friendship. Layern should be here. He's not with his family because he married me and brought me to the castle. I should have said no. He would be eating and enjoying himself, instead he's … I'm not sure where he is. No one has told me.

"Gemi, where is Layern staying?" I ask.

"I'm not sure, and if I did know, it would not be acceptable to tell you." He arches a brow. Gemi is truly a handsome man, and very sweet.

"It's unacceptable for him to be separated from his family," I say. My intention is not to be rude, but the table fails silent. Queen Nala opens her mouth to speak, but King Dramen places a berry in her mouth, and shakes his head 'no'. Then he speaks.

"My son, Prince Layern, is fine. You should not worry about him. He knows that after his punishment we will give him a homecoming celebration. You should think more on what type of celebration he will receive, one with you or one without."

I have no words, so I bow my head in respect and continue to eat. The chatter starts back up and everyone is eating, laughing and enjoying family time. I miss my mother, my father and Palmer too. He's my family now. I'm here among the Draglen family, but do I belong? I'm used to Earth. Kalin has been a place that I could only see by sneaking around. I always had to be careful, and could never stay long. I decide that if I can't see Layern, I'd better spend the time thinking. I eat in silence and let Layern's family enjoy meech.

***

After dinner, though Gemi and Beauka want to show me around, I ask if I can explore by myself. King Dramen assures me that the Queen will be busy and I will be safe. That gives me a sense of relief and I begin to walk the castle, exploring.

The castle is huge. My eyes don't know where to look. The colors, jewels, paintings, statues, and even the décor are amazing. I wish Layern were here. He would have me in some room doing nasty things to me. I wonder if Layern is thinking about me. It's not long before I find my room and climb into bed. A pattern quickly begins, with me waking up and eating breakfast with the family. Walking around until lunch. More walking. Maybe time with the women, and dinner, then bed. The night always ends with me crying, wanting Layern, my mother and even my own home. How did I get into this situation? Thirty fucking days is way too long!

TWO WEEKS LATER

LAYERN

Reseda cries every night, and I'm banned from my own home because I did something wrong in the family tradition. My mother and her secret are the cause of all this, not my marriage to Reseda! She was the victim in my mother's web. I'm tired of being in the woods. I have been trying to visit her secretly, but I'm being blocked by King Dramen, even in her dreams. I can see her, but that's it. I fucking miss touching her hair, lips… both lips, breasts and her afla. I don't want to swim any more. I'm liable to bed a mermaid if I don't get release soon. I need my Wella, she's my wife. We should have stayed for a longer honeymoon on Earth. FUCK!

I turn and see my brother, Draken.

"I'm here to check on you."

"Draken, just go, I don't need a fucking babysitter."

"I'll let that slide," Draken growls, "because under normal circumstances you would not speak to me in that manner unless you wanted to feel a little fire." I like him better when Cess is around.

"I'm fine, counting down the days. Why are you here and how did you find me?"

"You do know this will be my kingdom someday? I know where all my brothers go."

I stare at him, desperately wanting to be left alone, but no, he comes and takes a seat next to me on the ground.

"How's she doing?"

"She walks around the castle every day, and cries herself to sleep. Princess and Beauka have been trying to speak with her, but she's withdrawn."

"She needs me, brother, please talk with Father and have him lift the ban, and I will go to her tonight in her dream."

"Dreams are good, but what if I can get you two hours with her?"

I narrow my eyes and let my gift take over, only to find that Draken has indeed talked with Father, and has gotten me two hours with Reseda, but no one can know.

"When?"

"She will be here soon, Gemi is bringing her."

"Wait, she's flying on his back, that fucking…"

"That was a condition, brother. Our father was not pleased

about this, but he sees Reseda's sadness, too."

"Ok, thanks, I can't say thank you enough. Ok, you can leave. We don't need an audience."

"I can't leave, and neither can Gemi. We have to make sure it's two hours, and then take her away. You are capable of trying to run with her."

This is true, but I will never admit it.

"I will honor my father's wishes even if they are unfair."

"I'm done talking, I can smell Gemi flying close. Two hours, and we will be near. If you run, I will find you."

I ignore Draken as I can sense Reseda coming close. I feel like jumping up and down. I run into the cabin and clean a little, and make sure that everything is in place. I change slacks and hurry back outside to greet her. I'm granted the pleasure of seeing Gemi flying in with my Wella on his back. Though I'm jealous that her first ride on a dragon is with my very romantic brother, I know he would never betray me.

Gemi comes low and lands. Reseda jumps off his back and runs straight to me, leaping into the air. I catch her in my arms. I don't have time to thank my brother. I pull Reseda into my cabin.

"Oh, Lecena, I've missed you."

"I've missed you as well. You have been here in this place the entire time?"

"Yes, and as much as I'd like to talk with you, I need your body under mine."

She gives me a wicked grin and steps back, giving me a full

view of her blue dress. She slips out of it with ease, and she's wearing blue lace panties.

I look up and she's smiling, yes, my lecena knows me so well.

"You like?"

"I love, baby."

My body aches for her. I'm in her face fast, taking her head in my hands on the side of her face to kiss her gently. I would like to be rough, but she needs soft right now. I let one of my hands slide down her body, stopping at her breasts, pulling and pinching her nipples. Her moans and sighs are like music to my ears.

I'm not sure how or when we make it to the bed, but one of my hands is cupping her sex and the other is in her hair, holding it tightly. Pressing my fingers through the lace pushing it inside her, she moans loudly "Mmmmm!" My sex jumps at the sound of her moan. I rub hard, bringing my palm into direct contact with her clitoris, as my mouth ravishes hers. She's soon coming just like I want, and after her tremors are over, I rip the lace panties right off.

"Layern, I want you inside me, baby."

"I know, I need these panties, though, Seda," I say, dropping them on the table beside the bed. Quickly I remove my slacks, and with no hesitation I sink inside her comfort zone. "FUCK!"

I start a rhythm, circling, thrusting and slamming into Seda. I can't stop, I won't. My mouth finds her lovely neck, and I kiss and suck on her. Her nipples are hard and I can feel them rubbing against my chest. Lowering my head, I capture one with my mouth, biting softly and sucking. I slide to the other breast, not wanting any of her body neglected. We continue, until I flip onto my back, and now she's on top.

Seda face is beautiful as she feels the fullness of me inside her. Her hips begin to move and she's got the rhythm. I catch on quickly and our bodies are one. Her hands on my chest and mine on her hips, we move, just feeling each other in between our moans and growls. I've missed her so much. She pulls up slightly, only to slam back down onto me, damn that feels good.

"Do it again," I command.

Her breathing is fast. Her eyes are going from beast to human, but she does it again, giving us both our release. Her nails dig into my chest and I growl loud enough that I'm sure my brothers just want away from us both. She falls onto my chest and gives me a lazy kiss. I glance at the time, we have only about twenty minutes left.

"I don't want you to go," I say.

"I don't want to go, but I have to."

There is silence. She pulls herself off me and slides next to me, wrapping her leg around my body. I try to get a read on her, but she's blocking me, why?

"What's on your mind, Lecena?"

"I'm going back to Earth for these last two weeks."

"WHY?"

I'm in a panic. Why is she leaving? What has happened?

"Layern, I need to go home. I miss my home. I'm not part of your family."

"My family has not made you comfortable?"

If my family has been rude to her in any way I will leave this cabin and break all the rules. I will not tolerate any disrespect towards my Wella.

"Most of them are nice, but we did elope, and I don't want to be there without you. All I do is cry there."

"I will leave with you if you want. I will break my father's punishment to protect you, to be with you, Seda. Please don't leave."

"Layern, I spoke with your father. When I leave, you will be able to come back to the castle."

I frown in confusion. She's not telling me something.

"Tell me the truth, why are you leaving?"

Seda buries her face in my chest, taking deep breaths.

"I need to go home, say goodbye to Palmer and… go be with my mother and her family," she whispers. Her tears are coming down fast, and now I understand, she's decided to take my father's offer. I won't make her stay if she wants to leave. Why did she wait two weeks? My body is tense with anger. She doesn't love me, and now two women I have loved in my life have rejected me. I didn't have to be away from my home if she was going to leave.

I get up, not caring that her leg is on me I just push it away.

"Reseda, then why did you come here today?"

"I wanted to see you, Layern, I want us to be friends."

"I'm not fucking Palmer, and if you wanted to fuck you could have just said that."

I'm standing now, avoiding her eyes, putting on my slacks.

"That's harsh, Layern, and I know you are not Palmer. I just think we moved way too fast. I just got my freedom."

"Leave," I whisper.

"Huh?"

"I said get out, go and be with your mother and your boring life."

I feel awful for speaking this way to her, but she's broken my heart and I will not let her see me hurt. I can't believe this has happened to me. I'm glad she has her freedom, but I thought she would have chosen me over everyone.

Reseda climbs out of the bed, sobbing as she puts her dress back on. I turn and go into my bathroom, waiting for her to leave. I hear her approach the door.

"Layern, please don't do this."

I can't even speak, but I find more mean words.

"Reseda, it was fun, but you need to leave. I can go back to the castle. You get your freedom and so do I."

"What does that mean?"

"I could never have been truly faithful, I like variety, so go."

"You're an ass."

"I've had your ass, though, in many different ways. So I'm not an ass, but I do like fucking ass."

That should do it. I hate myself right now. The female I love, and married, wants to be friends with me. Palmer is her friend. Shit, anybody can be her friend! I'm her Molla, not a friend. I clench my teeth and I hear her crying, and then the door slams. When I know she has gone, I fall to the floor in disbelief. My Wella is gone. What have I done?

**

It's been a few days since I return to the castle. Since I gave the location of Reseda's mom to Gemi, her name has not been brought up. My mother is very happy. My father, though, seems a little down, and I think he enjoyed having Reseda around. I have been staying away from everyone, even choosing to eat in my room, but that hasn't stopped them from coming into my room to try to make me feel better. Fewton comes by nearly every day to see if I want to go and find some female company. Though I've been needing a release, Reseda is who I want. Not another female. My mouth made her hate me, I can't believe the way I talked to her, and she didn't deserve that. She deserved to have her freedom. To live with her family, not in fear of my mother. I may not be able to have her, and she may not want me, but if I find Palmer trying to lay one finger on her, I'm going to give him to some real killer females, mermaids.

RESEDA

What a stupid fool I was to believe Layern loved me. He was so cruel with his words. I would never have thought he could speak to me in such a way, but I was wrong. He basically said I was just a fuck. I've been thinking about how I'm going to get this marriage to him annulled. I'm sure he doesn't want word to get out, when he comes to Earth, that he has a wife. I'm free now. I could move anywhere in the world, or my mother and I can find a small place to live in Kalin. I love that choices are given to me. King Dramen saved me from Layern, and he had to know his son could be so cruel. I won't regret my decision to leave him. I do, however, regret falling in love. Now, the pain of not having him is so intense. The songs that have been written do not do justice to a broken heart. I have not eaten in two days, and only shower because I can't stand the smell. I called Palmer, and he insisted on coming over today. I don't want to see anyone, but Palmer is my friend. I just can't be totally honest with him. I'm sitting in my kitchen, on a stool, because it's too painful to sit at the table. I hear the knock at the door and know it's Palmer. Not feeling like getting up, I use my mind control and unlock the door.

"Reseda?" he asks, as if I'm a stranger.

"Yes, it's me."

"You look so sad. You have dark circles around your eyes. It's that guy, isn't it?"

I just nod at Palmer, words are difficult to form right now. I have them all in my head, but currently, voicing them is extremely hard. Palmer goes to the fridge, pulls out some juice and grabs some crackers.

"I know you may not know this, but you need nutrition. You look sick, Reseda. Drink this juice and eat a few crackers."

My eyelids are so heavy and my pupils hurt, but I find strength to square my shoulders, look him in the face and say, "NO!"

"Yes, I'm not sure what happened. You just disappeared and now you look… you look like you want to die, please eat."

"NOOO!"

"Ok, I will just place it in front of you and hope you pick up a cracker."

I don't care any more, secrets got me into this mess. I think it's time for Palmer to know the truth about me, and then maybe he will leave me the fuck alone.

"Palmer, when I need to eat I will. Yes, I require food every day or I do get sick, but that's mainly to do with the fact that dragons have to eat."

"See, this is why you need to eat, you didn't mean to say that."

"Say what? That I'm a dragon? I am a dragon, Palmer. If I wanted to, I could burn the entire city down."

"No, you couldn't."

He says that with a soft, but firm, voice. Why is he not running for the hills, or calling the hospital on me? I narrow my eyes at him, he knows something.

"Reseda, when my cousin came to town after your unexpected friend pushed me, she came to see if my suspicions were right."

"Go on."

"Well, she's a witch, or what my family likes to call the balance keeper."

I can't believe this.

"Are you… a witch?"

"Oh no, no… only the women are gifted with the gene in my family. The men are not."

"You mean to tell me you know I'm…"

"A dragon, yes, I do. I just found out, Reseda. Why have you never told me?"

"Get out of my house," I whisper.

"Reseda, I'm not scared. I still want to be your friend."

"Get out now and don't ever come back. We are not friends any more. Besides, I'm married."

"You're what? I'm not leaving."

I bite my lip, causing pain so that I will not spit fire. Palmer has no idea how dangerous I can be, or maybe he does, but I know my father always said to stay away from witches and anyone who would be around them. They have the ability to get the upper hand over dragons, just by using a few words.

"Leave my home, Palmer, this is my last time asking," I warn him.

He stares at me and walks towards me, and before I can hold back I breathe fire above his head and he falls to the ground. I'm so angry right now. I stand with my fists balled and ready to fight as his cousin comes in, holding her hand towards me. My body goes stiff, and a pain shoots through me like lava. This is why being around a witch is bad news. She holds me in my spot, preventing me from moving, as she helps Palmer up and they leave. I'm not released to move for what seems like forever, but is really only about five minutes. I receive a call from Noke, that my mother should be here soon with Gemi. He has been such a big help. Maybe I fell for the wrong brother. I stumble upstairs, making my way to the bed. Sleep is what I need.

***

My eyes open to bright sunshine. I see that my blinds are wide open. I never leave my blinds open. Rubbing my eyes, I notice fresh flowers all over my room. My sense of smell catches up with my sight, and they smell awesome. What day is it? I push myself forward, and that's when I see who's done this. The tears fall down my cheeks. This is the one person I can count on.

"You are finally awake, Reseda."

"It's really you?"

"Yes, now come give your homla a hug."

I jump out the bed wrapping my arms around my mother, crying non-stop. I've missed her so much, and now I can see her every day.

"Homla, homla, homla," I repeat, sobbing.

She will understand my pain. She was ripped away from her love, my father, at one time. I may not have been ripped away, but what choice did I have when Layern started saying all those evil things?

"I know, I know," She simply says. My mother is known as Dahee, I'm not sure of her real name, but this is what they call her.

We hug for a few more minutes before she points to the bathroom, and I just know things will be alright now. I take a long shower. Baths are such a reminder of Layern. I put on a loose dress and join my mother on the porch. She has iced tea waiting.

"Why iced tea?" I ask.

"This is what they drink in this part of Earth, right?"

I smile.

"Yes, Mom, they do."

"So tell me about Prince Layern, whom you married."

"There's nothing to tell. He married me to keep his mother, Queen Nala, from trying to kill you or me, that's it."

"That's it? I may not be young, but I'm smart enough, and

know enough about love, to see it was more than that. Reseda, you married him, shared his bed. You don't have to be strong for me."

I look out into the sky and think of Layern's smile, scent, and especially his touch. I crave his touch, my body aches for him. I have never spoken to my mother about any man. This could be uncomfortable.

"Yes, it was more than that, but he made it clear he was just doing me a favor."

"You believe him?"

"Yes, Homla, I do."

"He could have saved you in many different ways, Reseda. He chose to give you his name, something the Draglen men don't take lightly.

"He doesn't want me. He asked me to leave."

"You told him you wanted to be friends, though."

How the hell does she know that?

"How do you know what I said?"

"Gemi told me, and plus, I do know my daughter. Even if I couldn't see you like I should have."

Oh, that means that Layern told Gemi. Why would he mention I decided to leave? He didn't act like he even wanted me around. He basically told me I was a good fuck. If that's not clear about how someone feels about you, I don't know what is.

"Well, Gemi told you what Layern wanted you to know, he's not for me."

"Ok, I won't bring it up."

"Thank you."

"Now, who is this cute male named Palmer? He came over like five times while you slept." She grins.

I shake my head and start talking to my mother about Earth, telling her things she never knew. I plan on taking her to my shop. I've dreamed about having her in the store selling candles with me. We have a lot to catch up on, and Layern will soon be forgotten.

We spend the next week going to different places. We go on the ghost tour, eat tons of food, and she wants to see a real live alligator. Although it is hard to get close, as they are frightened of us. Palmer tries to come over so many times that my mother eventually lets him in. We talk, and I ask tons of questions about his family. He's fascinated about me being half-dragon. Palmer has gotten the message about only being friends, but sometimes I catch him staring at me with lust in his eyes.

Everything is going well until Gemi and Domlen show up at my door. I haven't seen Layern now in almost two weeks. They don't bother to knock, they just appear in the kitchen with me and my homla.

"Reseda, nice to see you again," Domlen says, calmly. "You have been asked to come to Cortamagen, and we're here to escort you there."

"What are you talking about? I have my freedom, which means I decline the invitation."

"Marilyn is in labor and she would like you there, as you are still considered Layern's Wella," Gemi says.

My mother is speechless. She looks at me as though she will stand behind me, whatever decision I make.

"I'm not Layern's Wella, and I'm sorry, I can't … I won't come back to Cortamagen."

"She is due any day now, Reseda, and she's begging for you to be there, please. Showken hates telling her bad news, and you saying no is like him telling her no. It will be bad for the entire castle if he gets angry," Gemi pleads.

"Why do you refuse?" Domlen asks.

I feel torn. I would love to see Marilyn's Young being born, but also that means seeing Layern. I'm not sure I can handle it right now. I frown as Gemi and Domlen wait for me to change my mind. I'm not ready to see Layern, but Marilyn is a human, having the second half breed, like me. I look at Domlen, and his eyes are narrow. Could he be upset with my reluctance to answer him?

"I refuse to go because that's not my family, I'm sorry."

Domlen begins to pace back and forth. Everyone is staring at him and he stops right in front of me, only a few inches away from my face.

"Reseda, I'm here at my brother's request, because his Wella wants you there. All my patience is gone. I don't like the word 'no', and if I have to drag you to Cortamagen by your hair, I will. Now, do you understand that my asking you was a courtesy?"

Shit, I think he has just told me I'm going whether I want to or not. I guess freedom does not mean really free. My mother's eyes are on me, and Gemi looks apologetic.

"How long do I have to get ready?"

"You are ready, let's go," Domlen says, irritated.

"Mom, stay here," I say, nodding. "I will be back as soon as the baby is born. I'm getting in Gemi's portal, you bully."

"There is no need for name calling, Reseda." Domlen's mood switches and he seems to be pleased about something.

Gemi opens his portal and we are off back to Kalin. It's not long before I'm back inside the castle, standing in a huge green room with paintings, flowers, food and a bed the size of three king-sized mattresses put together. I spot Marilyn instantly. She's wearing a green silk gown, her hair is pulled off her face and she's squeezing Showken's hand. I walk quickly over there, as she looks as though she is in pain.

"Oh, Reseda, I'm so glad you're here." Marilyn gives me a half smile.

"Shit, we are all glad you are here. Now you can take your turn with this screaming gorilla," Jazz says.

"You try delivering something that makes you breathe fire, before you judge."

Jazz holds up her hands in surrender, and I walk closer to see her. The room is filling up, I see Cess, Domlen, Draken, Hawken, Gemi, Fewton, Beauka, servants. This is entirely too many people. Layern is nowhere to be seen, but I'm sure he's near.

"Marilyn, what can I do for you?" I ask.

"Oh, Reseda, can you make all these people leave? I only want a few people right now."

I turn and look at everyone. The stares I receive inform me that this request will not happen.

"Well, Marilyn," I say, "I think you may need help, and should just ignore any faces you would rather not see right now."

Showken slides closer to her on the enormous bed, and I take a seat behind him.

"Mari," Jazz says, her hands on her hips, "if you want this room cleared out, maybe she can't get rid of them, but I'm not scared of them. I'll have them rolling out of here like a crazy lizard."

Cess is keeping her distance. Draken has wrapped his arms around her waist from behind, and it looks as though he's whispering to her. She's nodding.

The servants are placing cool towels on Marilyn's arms, legs and forehead.

"Thanks, Jazz, but I will keep everyone around. Reseda's right."

"Well, let me know if you change your mind," Jazz says, "because I don't give a rat's ass what these dragons think. This is your time."

Mari just nods, and I place a hand on her leg and start to rub it. She looks miserable. I can't believe I'm here for this birth. I'm nervous for two reasons. One, I have never seen a baby born, especially a unique Young like me, and second, I'm pretty sure Layern will come in soon.

The time moves slowly, and eventually people start leaving, I assume deciding to come in shifts. I hear some of the brothers talking, explaining that it's uncommon for a Young to take this long. I'm not sure of anything. After a while, Marilyn falls asleep, and that gives Showken a chance to speak with me. It's like he has been waiting.

"Reseda, such a pretty name. Tell me what my brother did to make you run?"

"What makes you think he did something?"

He gives me a huge grin, and those dimples, combined with his sexiness, are overwhelming. I lean back so I can breathe. Now I understand why Marilyn said 'no' to his helping me into the bath. I would have, too.

"Reseda, I'm the easy-going brother, and I can keep a secret too, so tell me what happened?"

"Your brother is an ass."

He bursts out laughing, bending over until I find myself laughing with him. I don't think I've laughed like this since being with Layern.

"We are all asses, Reseda. That's a tradition among us Draglens. That includes my sweet sister Beauka, but please, describe how he was an ass this time."

"Thanks for making me laugh, Showken, I needed that. Your brother basically told me I was a fuck, nothing more."

"He said that?"

"Well, yes."

"I wonder why he would say that when he loves you. Reseda,

could he have lashed out because you chose to leave?"

"I'm here for Marilyn. Discussing Layern was not part of the deal, and I can always go home."

"Whoa, please don't leave. You've never seen Marilyn angry, and for some odd reason her fire-breathing is powerful. Sorry. If you don't want to talk about how my brother loves you, then I will back off."

He's right. They are all asses. His sarcasm is unnecessary. I roll my eyes, and he smiles again. Oh boy, he's used to getting away with shit with that smile. I shake my head and decide to get myself some food from the enormous buffet set out. I'm reaching for some berries when suddenly I feel Layern behind me.

"You should try the blue berries. They have a different taste than on Earth."

"No, thanks. I think I'll eat the red and yellow ones."

He comes close and his chest is against my back. I gasp at how my body comes to attention at his presence. He leans down, pressing a soft kiss on my neck.

"I think you would like blue berries, and you would wound me if you don't give them a try."

"I have and they are not that good. In fact, I usually have to mix them with another berry."

"Really, I think you lie."

"I don't care what you think, Prince Layern."

"Seda, we need to talk."

"We talked. You remember? 'You fuck ass,' were your words

to me, and then you told me to leave. I think we have done enough talking."

"I think I'm an ass and we should talk, please, I… just let me talk with you, ok?"

"I'm here for Marilyn, and as soon as her Young is born, I'm going home."

He wraps his arms around my waist and holds me tight, pressing his hard body against mine. I try to push away, but he feels so good. I should be cursing him for speaking to me the way he did, but here I stand, getting wet and weak in the knees for him.

"I just want to talk, please."

"Prince…"

"Don't hurt me, I'm just Layern to you, always."

"I don't think it will be the same between us, Layern. You said some harsh things and I… I didn't choose love."

"Lecena, please give me a chance to make it up?"

I am about to say it's too late, when Marilyn wakes with a piercing scream. The room quickly fills with all the family, including King Dramen and Queen Nala.

"IT'S COMING!" Marilyn yells.

The servants get her up, and Showken goes down by her legs and slowly pushes up her gown. All the brothers are behind the bed, and the only ones who can see Marilyn's sex are Showken and King Dramen.

"Reseda, Jazz… please, each one of you take my hand."

"Mari, shit! I don't have dragon in me. Don't break my damn

hand."

I don't speak. I go to her left side, holding her hand, and Jazz goes to the right. I know from reading the history of Cortamagen that the men deliver their own children. The females are to support the mother.

Showken's skin looks green. I turn and see all the brothers looking frightened. I'm guessing this will be the first time they have seen a Young being born.

"This is a time of joy," King Dramen says. "Our first descendant of the next Draglen blood is being born. My son Showken, I will help guide you this first time, but all other times you will birth your Young yourself. The first touch they feel, first voice they hear and first set of eyes they see will be yours."

Showken doesn't say anything, just nods.

"If you don't get this baby out of me now, I'm going to kill you both!" Marilyn says through clenched teeth.

She's holding my hand pretty tight, so I think it would be a good idea.

"My son, give your Wella something to calm her." King Dramen says.

Showken comes beside me, leans down over Marilyn and gives her a deep kiss, releasing a light green fog which just covers her body. It looks so intimate and hot. I squeeze my legs together and I'm turned on. My head turns around slightly and my eyes meet Layern's. He feels it too.

Showken goes back down between Marilyn's legs. He and

King Dramen dip low, and they are speaking Magen now. Everyone in the room is silent, including Marilyn. Well, except for an occasional moan. I can hear her body stretching, but she still looks relaxed. Showken lifts his head. He's sweating profusely and his eyes are wide. King Dramen pulls him back down.

I hear some of the brothers talking."That looks very difficult," Domlen says. "It's beautiful," Gemi smiles." I'm not doing that," Hawken says. "I don't see Youngs in my future," Warton says. "I'm going to have lots of Youngs," Draken says. "I'll have a Young if I can have the love of my life back," Layern says.

"Shhh." Beauka hisses.

"She should have gotten pregnant by a human, this shit is for the birds," Jazz says.

"I said shh, and that includes you, Jazz."

"I'm not scared of you, Beauka."

"Both of you, please," I say.

King Dramen sticks his head up.

"It's almost here. Nala, we will be drangrands."

This is how I should have been born, but my father says I was born in the woods, and he could not help my mother's pain. Why couldn't I have this love around me at my birth, instead of hate and secrecy? Maybe coming here was a bad idea. Marilyn deserves this, but so did my mother and I.

There is no pushing. They are waiting for the Young to come through the passage. It's not long before Showken comes up holding a green, slimy shell smiling a perfect smile. The Young punches through the shell and Showken helps peel the shell off, finally we will know the sex.

"It's a boy!" Showken yells.

The room erupts into applause, but we hear two thuds as bodies drop to the floor. I look around and Hawken is missing, and so is Fewton. I smile to myself.

"Let me hold him, Showken!" Marilyn says, crying.

He cleans the baby, and King Dramen collects all the shell pieces and places them in a jewel box with emeralds on the outside. Showken places the Young in Marilyn's arms. I get a chance to look at the Young, and he's gorgeous, - green eyes with a hint of hazel, blond hair and dimples. Wow, he's going to be handsome.

"Hi, little guy, I'm your momma," Marilyn says. This is so beautiful. She has all this love, family, husband, and now a child. I start to walk away, but she stops me. Showken has sat down next to her, speaking to the child in Magen, and the Young is smiling.

"Reseda, Showken and I want you to be our baby's godmother. I know that over in Kalin this is unheard of, but you are just like him. What better person to teach him how to be both human and dragon?"

I'm in shock. I can't accept this, can I? Oh, wow, this is such an honor. Layern walks straight to me.

"Congratulations, Seda," he whispers in my ear. Queen Nala looks distraught.

"What about Jazz, she's your best friend?"

"I'm ok with it, Reseda, besides, I can't fly. Now say yes, damn it."

Everyone starts laughing, including me. I walk over to Marilyn and give her a kiss. She lifts the Young and places him in my arms, and I'm overcome with emotion. The tears roll like a river. I have something to love. A real half-breed like me. Layern comes and stands next to me along with his brothers as we all look at the handsome dragon Young.

Everyone takes a turn with the baby. I notice he has not yet been given a name yet.

"What is his name, Marilyn?" I ask.

"Showken and I decided to combine our names. So his name is Showlyn, he has both our names!" she smiles.

"It's perfect, beautiful," I respond.

I try to sneak out of the room, but Layern is right behind me. I don't know what possesses me to run, but I do, and he laughs and starts chasing me. He is on my heels and I pick up the speed, turning corners and enjoying the chase.

"I'm going to catch you, Seda," he says, and turns off, going down another hall. Damn. I bite my lip, trying to think of my next move. I take off, running back towards the room, but I'm pulled into another room. The door shuts, and there stands Layern, smiling.

"Why did you run?"

I back away, and realize I'm in his room. How did I not see that coming?

"I'm not sure. Running seemed like my only option."

"I want you, and you want me. I can smell your arousal."

The chase was exciting, and I do want him.

"You are my wife still, are you going to deny me your pleasure? I've been with no other."

"Layern, I don't think this will work. Besides, your mother hates me."

"I love you."

"Layern, my mother is waiting at home."

"I'll send for her. I love you."

I sigh as he comes close and starts kissing me. I try to keep my mouth closed, but he works his tongue over my lips, coaxing me to open, and soon I'm lost. Layern has my heart, and though I should run again, I step back and remove my dress. He smiles as he sees I'm wearing no panties.

"You finally learned, Lecena."

He doesn't give me a chance to speak. He's in my face, hands on my ass, squeezing hard. Our lips are all over each other. His hands are in my hair and I wrap a leg around his waist. He walks backwards with me to his bed, placing me on my back.

"Open your legs wide for me, like the lecena you are."

My legs fall apart and his finger slowly slides up and down my folds. He opens me and slides his finger over my clitoris, and I moan "Mmmmm, YES!" I'm pulling the pillow behind me so hard it rips apart. He doesn't stop the torture, taking his finger to his mouth and sucking hard. He does it again. This time he places his finger at my mouth for me to open and I do, and suck, tasting my own juice.

His lips touch every part of me, front to back, before he slides inside me, and I can't hold on any longer from all the foreplay. I explode immediately. We move slowly. Not rushing, taking our time, and with each thrust he tells me he needs me, he can't live without me. The words send me over again, and soon Layern finds his orgasm.

I fall asleep in his arms, forgetting everything just for this moment.

LAYERN

This is the first time I've been happy in almost two weeks. I have my lecena in my arms and I'm never letting her go. If she doesn't want to live here, I will go anywhere she wants. I just want to be with her. She looks beautiful. She's right. My mother hates her, but it's not my mother's choice. Besides, this all started because of love. I smell my scent on Reseda, and it's the best mixed with hers. I don't want to leave this bed. I slide out of the bed and call Gemi, asking if he can go check on Reseda's mom and let her know everything will be ok. Gemi agrees without hesitation. There will be a celebration today for Showlyn. I want Reseda to stay so I can announce my choice to stay with her, even if that means leaving the castle.

I have servants bring in food for us, so we can stay in this room until evening for the celebration. I start running her a bath, pouring some of my oil in there for her. I feel a push in my head from Draken, and I reject him. He pushes harder this time, almost knocking me off my feet.

"WHAT?"

"Cess wanted to know if Reseda's going to come to the celebration."

"I'm not sure, but I'll ask," I say, pushing him out.

Draken stops pushing and I'm left alone in the bathroom, leaving me to attend to my Seda. I climb into bed next to her, planting kisses on her, waking her up. She starts moving, making the sweetest sound ever.

"Layern, I'm sleepy and sore."

"I know, the bath is ready," I say, standing and picking up her naked body. I walk into the bathroom and place her in the water, and I see her wince from pain. She will be fine soon. I slide off my slacks and climb in behind her, taking the sponge off the shelf and squeezing water over her breasts. I love taking care of her, she's everything I need, and I'll forever regret saying all those mean things to her.

"Lay your head back on my shoulder."

"Mmm…"

I chuckle, because she's tired, I need her more alert, this day will be spent in our bedroom.

"Layern, what are we doing?"

"Taking a bath."

She splashes water.

"I mean, me in your bed, bath, and your home… nothing has

changed."

"Everything has changed, lecena. I expected you to give up everything for me, but I now know I'm willing to give up anything for you, including Cortamagen."

"Wait, Layern, why? You love it here."

"I love you more. I know you don't want to be around my mother, and you shouldn't be in an environment that could be dangerous."

"Layern-"

"Seda, I'm not leaving your side, and I will spend a lifetime making up to you all the horrible things I said, and what my mother has done to you."

"You don't have to do this."

"Ok, let's not talk about that, how about we make love in this bath."

She moans in agreement and that's enough to get my sex hard and ready for her comfort zone. I lift her up and slide inside her from the back, positioning her where she can lean over and hold onto my thighs as I take her again.

We make love in the bath twice before we decide to shower and clean our bodies. We lie in bed and talk, eat and make love. This is the honeymoon we should have been enjoying.

I'm not going to be separated from my lecena ever again. My mother and my father have separated us, and I understand my father's reason, but my mother is just a woman who didn't get the male she wanted. Reseda has been a victim all her life, and I will not allow her to be touched again. I love my home, my brothers and sister, but I will leave to keep my Wella safe.

***

The evening comes quickly, and I've not heard back from Gemi yet. I'm sure everything is ok. It's just that I worry about my brother, the voice of reason is what we all call him. Reseda decides to stay and celebrate Showken and Marilyn's Young. She chooses a short, blue dress. Very unusual here, but she has great legs and I will enjoy watching them. We walk out of the room, and we are greeted by Gemi.

"We need to talk, right now," he says.

"What's wrong?"

I try to get a read on him, but his nervousness is overpowering the real problem.

"Ok, Seda, can you give me one minute?"

"Yes, of course."

She walks a little way down the hall and pauses, looking out of the window, and I admire her for a few seconds before turning my attention back to Gemi.

"What's wrong, brother?"

"We have a problem. Palmer's cousin is a witch, and she knows who we are, without a doubt."

Gemi and I whisper low enough that Seda can't hear this. If that female is a witch, that causes another serious issue.

"What about Palmer? He must not be involved. He never used any power against me."

"No, he can't practice, and they call themselves 'balance of the Earth' now, but she's feisty."

"How do you know this?"

He doesn't speak, he just looks at me, and I get a read on him. This nut has fallen for her. She could do him serious harm.

"Gemi, I know I don't have room to say anything about this, but brother, she's got the ability to hurt you."

"I know, but she makes me feel alive. The problem is she's protecting Reseda's mother for Palmer, which is how I found out she was a witch. She kind of brought me to my knees."

"Shit, brother, I'm sorry. I should have come with you. I see the problem. I'll figure out something. Stay away from her for now, until we can figure out how to handle this."

"I'm not sure I can do that, but I will try," he says, walking away. I'm hoping the read I just picked up was not true, it's like a suicide mission. My lecena is still looking out the window, smiling. She looks beautiful.

"What's making you smile?"

"There is such peacefulness out in the fields. Everyone is getting along, laughing and preparing for the celebration of a new prince among the Draglen family. Amazing!"

I don't respond. She's just enjoying. Although she's in this family too, I just might have to move.

"You ready to dance?"

"Oh, I'm always ready to dance."

We walk hand and hand to the sound of drums and cymbals. This music will play for days, giving everyone a chance to dance as often as possible for the new Young. The closer we get to the music and fun, the higher I can feel her anxiety getting, but my father has assured me that Reseda will be fine. We finally make it to the other side of the castle, which has giant, clear doors with specks of jewels of the color of each family member. In honor of Showken and Marilyn producing the first Young for the next generation, the theme will center on emeralds.

"Fun is the only option you have," I say. She returns a huge grin, and we walk into a room of people full of life, dancing, laughing and playing instruments. My family has our seats next to Showken and Marilyn. The Young, Showlyn, is in the arms of my mother, Queen Nala. The night should be fun. We take our seats unnoticed by my family, except for the King and Queen. My brothers are either dancing, eating, or having fun with their Wellas or other females. Beauka is quiet, though. She seems sad. I'm not even going to try to find out. She's complicated.

"You hungry?"

"No."

"What's wrong?"

"Nothing, well maybe I'm in the castle, the place where I was banned or to be killed. I feel a little uneasy."

"Don't worry, you need some wine. Wine for my Wella!" I shout.

She blushes, making me smile. Yes the decision to be with her forever is my only option.

After a few cups of wine, and some fruit and a little bit of kissing, I convince her to dance with me. We walk out into the crowd of dancing people and I can hear them talking. I'm the best dancer, but Seda can keep up with me. I think Cess could too, but Draken doesn't allow her even to be touched.

The music starts to slow down, and Seda and I take advantage and move closer, letting our bodies go down low, and returning up very slowly. Her body feels the beat and we start to circle each other, and she gives me a smile. I think she's challenging me. I narrow my eyes and she grins more. Yes, she wants to play. The music starts to increase in speed, and so does our dancing. Reaching for her hand, I pull her closer and give her a little grind before I really start to dance, making my way around her, even finding time to plant a quick kiss on her neck.

Seda is no pushover, though. She drops low and dances seductively in that position, causing males, including a few of my brothers, to smile, maybe wanting more than to watch her dance, but she's mine. Her hips move like the music, and her legs are around my waist, off my waist and even on the ground as she shows off her skills. We are the perfect match. I swing her my way, and it's more provocative than any dance you can imagine. My hands rub her like we are alone. Her mouth opens as my hands glide down her ass, rubbing it up and down, giving it a squeeze. We continue our dance and move right into a few more songs before hunger becomes a need.

"Food?"

"Oh yes, please, I'm starved."

"Come, I can't have you starving."

We take our seats, and we're greeted by servants. We each take a little of everything, including the many different cupcakes that Showken has demanded. Seda and I enjoy our time with each other while everyone takes his turn with the newest member of the family, Showlyn. We sit and watch as my brothers dance with the women, except for Warton. He doesn't like to dance, although he can dance if he really wants to. I'm going to miss this, my brothers, family. Dancing and celebrating is always fun, but I can't ask Seda to live here with my mother, and besides, she wants to have contact with her mother always. I can move wherever she chooses.

"Layern, what are you thinking about?"

"I'm thinking of how I can't wait to get you back to the room, or the hall. Maybe I could walk you right over to the swing and sit you on my lap."

She giggles and I like that sound. It's interrupted by my mother, Queen Nala.

"My son, the one who shares part of my gifts, please come walk with me?" she asks, smiling. I know better. Though she loves her Youngs, Queen Nala can be dangerous if pushed.

Marilyn gets up, takes Showlyn out of Queen Nala arms and gives him to Seda, who looks terrified and amazed at the same time. Showlyn and Seda are the same, the only two of their kind.

She looks at me and gives me a nod. I glance at my mother who has now turned her back, waiting for me to escort her as we walk.

"Showken, don't..."

"Brother, this is my Young celebration, if anything goes wrong a green monster will appear, and no one will stop me. She's safe." Showken grins.

I stand and lean down, giving a kiss to Seda, and one to Showlyn, on his forehead. I notice his alertness, and the heat coming off his body. A Young in the castle will be fun for us all. Well, for everyone else. I stand, taking a few steps, placing myself right next to my mother. I take her arm in mine, and we walk down the stairs to the right, which lead into a garden.

"My son, Layern, you can relax, I will not choke you."

"I know, because my father has given you an order."

"Let's not get into the reasons why I'm not choking you. The focus is that I'm not going to choke you."

"Why are we walking?" I ask.

"I think you need to hear my side of the story, so you can understand my anger."

"Queen-"

"Listen, my son, please?"

Damn, she said please, maybe I can give her the benefit of the doubt.

"Ok, I will listen."

"Many moons ago, your father, King Dramen, was just a prince, and I was an advisor to Queen Mija, your drangrand." She sighs. We head further into the garden that leads to the water. "Prince Dramen and I were in love. I knew the customs, but I was young, and assumed I would be his only. The ceremony was great and our union was perfect, until he took a Giver. I had already had three Youngs and he got bored. It lasted for ten years and then we were back having more Youngs, but he informed me he was taking another Giver, and this time my anger could not be contained. I felt ashamed, knowing my Molla was with another, so I killed the second one. He only became angry and took on three more, and I killed them. Your father is stubborn, so eventually I gave up. I became numb to the Givers, and my heart turned black and hard. All my love was toward my Youngs, no one else. Then my friend and I decided to visit Earth. I left you and your brothers with some servants, and went to Earth for about three months. During that time, we both met Reseda's father. He had red hair and was handsome. He didn't know what we were, but we both wanted this man, but decided to save our friendship. We made a blood seal that neither one of us would have him."

She stops talking for a few minutes, then starts speaking again. I don't say anything, it's best to let her talk without questions.

"Apparently, my friend didn't keep her promise after we returned back home. She continued to go back because he loved her. It wasn't long before she became pregnant. I thought she would get rid of the baby. In fact, that was the plan, but it was a lie. The only friend I had betrayed me. Your father was into himself, back then, and my heart broke, and when I put the pieces together, it was solid and unbreakable. When the Young was born, I didn't lay my eyes on her. Just gave the ruling, your father agreed as he was too busy with his Givers at the time. I feel your confusion about why I'm telling you this. I will not ever be close to your... whatever you want to call her, but I will not come after her if she's your choice, don't leave your home."

She lays this on me, after I have made my decision to leave, and now I see how angry and hurtful this can be. I mean, my cousin had sex with a female I wanted as my Wella, and I took his head off his body. I guess I'm no different from my mother. We both love hard, and when we are hurt, we go to extremes.

"My Wella. Yes, my Wella has to feel comfortable and you don't speak, just look at her. She reminds you of her father. You will always look at her with hate and pain, and she is the daughter of a man you wanted. How do I deal with that?"

"My son, it may take more time, but I would rather have my son in his home than gone. I have nothing without my Youngs. Every one of you has kept me going, and if I didn't have you I would have been a dark dragon without any regard for life."

"This is something I have to think about. Seda is my love, and I love my family, but I love her more. I will consider your offer, but thank you for sharing that with me, Queen Nala."

We both smile, embrace and walk back to the celebration to continue partying. This walk has given me a better knowledge of how to deal with this situation. This thing is not changing my love for Seda, my lecena.

RESEDA

Finally, Layern returns with his mother. She doesn't look my way, but Layern comes straight for me. What did she say? He is smiling and seems calm, but that doesn't mean she hasn't said something that could put my life at risk. Beauka comes over and takes Showlyn from my arms. Layern stands in front of me and holds out his hand, and without hesitating I take it and stand with him. He looks at Showken and gives him a nod and a huge grin.

"I need everyone's attention, please," Layern shouts. His voice carries, and the drums, laughter and movements all stop. He has everyone's attention, including mine. What is he doing?

He walks us both to the front of the crowd, and now everyone can see us, and all my insides are flipping out of control. "Relax, Seda," he whispers. I squeeze his hand in protest.

"What are you doing?" I ask, quietly.

He ignores me, and addresses the people and his family.

"I'm sure everyone knows I took a Wella on Earth. Here she stands next to me, and her name is Reseda. I ask my family and the people of Cortamagen to forgive me for taking on a Wella in a non-traditional way. I do have to say that I love her with all my heart and would do anything to make her happy. That's why I'm considering leaving Cortamagen, and joining my Wella in a place she will love. I love you all, especially my brothers and my sister. I hope everyone will give Reseda and me time to think this through and, whatever decision we make, that it will be celebrated and not mourned. Thank you."

The silence is scary, and then I hear Gemi yell.

"Music, he's done with his announcement, carry on."

The looks I start to get are of confusion, anger, jealousy and happiness. The celebration starts back up, and Cess and Marilyn are at my side, pulling me away from Layern. He smiles, and I walk away to talk with them.

"You're leaving, you can't leave," Marilyn says.

"Why do you want to leave? Cess asks. I mean, I know Queen Nala is a handful, but nothing bad will happen to you. Draken will see to it, and so will I."

Before I can speak, Jazz has joined us, and her response is... different.

"Well, fuck me running. I didn't see that shit coming. Reseda, you got that booty to make a dragon leave his castle. I need a lesson."

We all just look at her. I guess I'm not the only one shocked at her speech.

"Ladies, it's very touching how you have accepted me, but the Queen in this castle doesn't want me here, and though you have welcomed me, she is still the Queen."

"Cess will be queen," Jazz says, "Then she will be a guest. I say stay and see what happens." Marilyn nods in agreement. I look down and see Bruiser hanging around Marilyn.

"Well," I say. "Like Layern said, we are discussing all the options."

The ladies change the subject, and it's all about the Young. I'm relieved to have the attention off me. This is what I wanted to avoid. I don't want Layern to give his family up for me, it's just wrong. Layern and I must talk, he didn't tell me about this announcement. Now I'm backed into a corner.

The ladies and I talk more, but soon I find myself on the dance floor, and this time Gemi joins me, and he, I and Layern have the best sex dance threesome ever. Well, not really sex, but I wanted to come. Layern and I celebrate the entire night with wine, food and dancing. I even get to see Layern and his brothers all change into dragons as they fly above us, blowing fire so Showlyn can see, and he loves it. He somehow knows this is for him.

***

The sun starts to rise, and finally we are standing in Layern's room. He looks at me and smiles, pulling me close.

"Why the speech, Layern? And why didn't I know anything about it?"

"I told you that I was going to follow you, Seda. I had already informed my brothers and sister. The time was right to announce you as my Wella, and to announce the plan to leave."

"I'm not sure I want you to leave your family."

"I'm sure I'm not living without you," he says. "Listen, it's been a long night and we need sleep before we party today. So let's just make love and then sleep, ok?"

He gives me a silly grin, and I can't help but laugh. I'm tired as well, but all that dancing has made me hot, and I need him inside me. Maybe after some hot sex and some sleep we can revisit this conversation. I will have to remember that he has a way of avoiding my questions. I'm sure he knows what he's doing. He pushes me back on the bed and rips off the dress, and it's not long before I'm lost in making love to my Molla.

***

The sun is shining brightly. The windows are open, with flowers and birds chirping on the edge. It's a beautiful sight. Layern's eyes are open, watching me carefully.

"Should I say good morning, or afternoon?"

"It's afternoon, Lecena."

"So, are we going to talk?"

"Ahh, here you go again with trying to talk about something

that has already been made final."

"Really? I don't get to express my concerns, or even have a choice in this matter?"

"Not if you are trying to convince me to leave you and stay home."

"Layern, we need to discuss what will be best. You know, leaving the only family you have ever known, that's not going to be easy."

"You are my family too, Seda, and I'm not living without you, and you shouldn't be in a place where my mother issued a ban on you."

"Well, I need to get home to my mother."

"Oh, umm, about that. It seems Palmer's cousin is protecting her from us. Did you know she was a witch?"

Shit! I forgot to tell him that, but that would make him even more determined to keep Palmer away from me. Maybe she's protecting my mother for me? I don't ask though. My mother is a dragon. I'm not worried about her being attacked on Earth, she's the predator, not the prey.

"I... I just recently discovered that Palmer's cousin is a witch. Well, that the women in his family are, but not the men."

"You didn't think to tell me, knowing how dangerous a witch can be to our kind? Gemi went there and was subjected to her skills."

"I'm sorry, I should have told you. It slipped my mind. Is Gemi ok?"

"Yes, he's fine, but he didn't get a chance to see your mother."

"I will leave today and go home, and check on my mother and my store."

"The celebration is still going on, though."

"Yes, I know, Layern, but I need to talk with my mother, alone."

He narrows his eyes and his beast comes forth yelling.

"NO!"

"I'm not saying I don't want to be with you. I just want to have some time with my mother, just like you talked with Queen Nala alone yesterday, and I deserve to have that as well."

"That's different. You were at the celebration too, and I didn't leave the planet to talk with her. You are going back to Earth, with, remember, a witch who knows what you are. They hate our kind."

"Palmer is my friend, he wouldn't allow anything to happen to me or my mother."

"Palmer wants to fuck you, multiple times."

"You think so little of me," I say through clenched teeth, "that, because Palmer wants to fuck me, as you so bluntly put, it that I will give in. I'm not the one with a reputation for having numerous women, sometimes the same night."

He looks shocked and apologetic, but I'm pissed. He can't assume, because someone wants me, that I want them, and if he wants a relationship with me then trust is a must, or we can call this off.

"Seda, I'm sorry, please forgive me. I... I just go a little crazy when I've felt his thoughts and know what he wants from you. It's taking all my energy not to kill him, and trust me when I tell you I have killed before."

"Your 'sorry' sounds like an excuse for your remarks and behavior."

"Ok, you want to go see your mother alone, I want to be near you. If you go, do you promise to be back in twenty-four hours?"

"Twenty-four hours, Layern, really?"

"Lecena, I don't trust the witch, so twenty-four hours, or I'm coming to get you, and if the witch gets in my way, well you already know what I will do."

My husband is crazy, there's no getting around this.

"Well, since you want to go, I need some sweet pie to hold me over."

My body stands to attention at his words. His hand cups my breast, and involuntarily I moan, "Mmm." Layern knows how to get to me every time. I can't even respond; as his hands go to work on my body, my anger slips away. His hands are like magic, touching every spot to make my body squirm. He watches me intensely as he slides inside me, making my legs tremble.

"I love you," he whispers, as his tongue dips into my ear.

"Mmmm... Yes!"

I will get ready for home in a few hours, but for right now I will enjoy the pleasure of Layern, and give him some pleasure too.

***

I'm bathed and dressed, ready to go back to Earth and see my mother. Layern and I are in an embrace when there is a knock on the door.

"It's Gemi and Hawken," he says.

I nod, and he goes to answer.

"We have a huge problem," Hawken says, pushing his way into the room. "You and your Wella should get ready."

"Hawken, what are you talking about?" Layern growls. I'm assuming Hawken is not his favorite brother.

"Well, Reseda's mother is here, as in the castle, in Gemi's room, along with a witch. Yes, a fucking witch!"

Layern turns and looks at me, and my eyes are about to pop out of my head, but I soon gain composure.

"Where is your room, Gemi?"

"Wait, you are not going to his room. We will bring your mother in here." Layern frowns.

Gemi holds up his hands, pleading with us both to stop speaking.

"She can't leave the room. The witch put a spell on my room to protect her and Reseda's mother."

"WHAT THE FUCK HAPPENED, GEMI?" Layern yells, causing items in his room to hit the floor.

"Don't yell at me, brother! Your Wella's mother insisted on coming, and the witch insisted she come to protect Reseda's mom."

Layern starts pacing the floor. He stops and stares at us all, and resumes pacing. He starts speaking Magen, and I'm sure he is saying foul words.

"I need to see my mother," I say. "I was on my way back to see her."

"Seda, it's a witch in there with her."

"Palmer wouldn't let her hurt me."

"Did you hear either of my brothers mention that Palmer was here? That means new rules may apply here."

"Well, I'm going to Gemi's room, then."

"Seda, you are trying my patience. I will have to go with you, then."

We walk quickly to Gemi's room, not saying a word. I can feel Hawken's and Gemi's presence behind us. I've never encountered a witch, but in history dragons don't like them, as their power can sometimes get the best of us. We arrive at Gemi's room, and Layern opens the door. I rush in, and see my mother staring out the window.

"Homla?"

"Reseda, are you ok?" My mother says, walking towards me.

She gives me a hug and a kiss.

"Yes, why did you come here? You know the danger you are in?"

That's when the witch comes walking out of the bathroom looking beautiful, her hair is flawless. She looks like a goddess. I glance at Layern to make sure his eyes stay on me, but Gemi's eyes are roaming her body.

"She has nothing to fear. I have her very well protected. Nice to see you again, Reseda," she says. I don't remember her name, nor do I care.

"What did you come here for? I was leaving, on my way home to you."

"That's why I'm here. I would like to speak with my Young alone," my mother says.

"Hell no, no, it's not going to happen. This witch could be planning to steal her. I'm not leaving." Layern's voice is stern.

"She will be fine, little dragon," the witch says. It's funny how she says it, and I almost giggle, but I contain myself.

"Call me 'little' one more time, I will call in some forces that not even you and your tricks will be able to handle," Layern snarls.

"Ok, listen," my mother says, calmly. "I just want to talk with Reseda, Prince Layern. I know she loves you. I would never steal her away."

There is a stare-down for what seems like forever. Hawken and Gemi don't say anything. Hawken looks on guard, but Gemi is relaxed.

"If I step out, the witch comes out too."

"Layern, she can't hang around the castle. If anyone finds out..." Hawken says, stressing.

"Listen, I'm only giving her mother five minutes, and if you say anything about this witch in the castle, before we all die, I will kill you first."

Gemi opens the door as if everything is settled. Layern walks over to me, sticks his tongue in my mouth and claims me, right in front of everyone. He lets everyone walk out before he closes the door behind us. I look at my mother, and we both walk over to a grey lounge.

"Reseda, I love you and I'm so happy you have found love." She pauses. "I knew love like that once before with your father, but things got in the way and we were separated. I don't want that for you."

"What are you saying?"

"I'm saying be with your husband, Reseda, not me. I will be fine, I've been around a lot longer than you, and now that you are free, you can come and see me."

"I don't understand, what are you saying, please, I can't lose you."

"Oh, my daughter, you could never lose me, we will get to see each other more, but I belong in Noke, and you belong here in the castle, as a princess."

I begin to cry, because my homla is giving me the ok to be with Layern. She has to know the problem is with Queen Nala, not me.

"I understand what you are trying to do, but Queen Nala would never let me stay."

"Yes she will, I know her very well, and she loves her Youngs and will put aside her feelings to ensure their happiness, just as I would do for you. I don't want you living with me to make up lost time, we have many years ahead to spend time together, and besides, I want you to have Youngs."

We embrace, and now we are both crying. I love my homla very much, and can't imagine life without her.

"Now, call your Molla in, so I can get a good look at him."

I wipe my face and yell for Layern. He's in the room before I can finish his name.

"Layern, this is my homla, and she gives us her blessing to live as one."

"Nice to meet you, I'm glad you don't judge me based on my mother's actions."

"Your mother and I will have our day, but for now, I will be returning to Noke. If you can promise to bring my daughter to Noke often, I will be on my way. I'm sure it won't be long before Nala feels my presence."

"Yes, of course," he says. "I will bring her to you as often as you like."

"Layern, wait. Your mother doesn't want me here."

"She will not give you any problems, Reseda, trust me."

My mother stands and gives me another hug and kiss, and then does the same to Layern. She and the witch leave, in a portal my mother has. I didn't know she could even use a portal.

I turn and look at Layern, he has a huge grin, and those blue eyes are sparkling.

"I guess we can stay if you want."

"Come here, Lecena, I'm going to take care of you forever.

Now let's get some things together."

"We have to wait to have a traditional union here, everyone is celebrating Showlyn."

"We are going to come together tonight, Seda, and I will fly with you."

"Layern, I don't know how to transform into a dragon, I've never done it before."

"You will tonight."

***

Since Layern found out that I would stay in the castle with him, he has been busy with his brothers all day. Cess, Beauka and Jazz have been with me all day, doing my hair, makeup and even finding me the perfect blue gown. It won't be like they normally do a union, but I will take him on completely.

The day is filled with fun in Layern's room. The ladies, except for Marilyn, stay with me the entire day. Jazz tells me how much Marilyn wanted to be with us, but she and Showken are getting ready for more celebrating about the new baby.

"Oh, Reseda, don't get knocked up like Marilyn!" She gleams. I like Jazz. She's so open and blunt.

"I'm happy to have another sister," Beauka says, "And also to see my brother Layern smiling again. We never thought he would love again." Beauka is the real princess in this castle, and it shows. Her class, grace and beauty are amazing.

"Well," Cess says. "I'm so happy you will be living in the castle with us. Everyone loves Layern, and now we all love you as well. Maybe not Queen Nala, sorry, Beauka." I've heard Cess has great dancing skills. I will only see her dance with Draken, though, and rumor has it that no one is allowed to touch her.

We talk and laugh and soon it is time to go to the celebration. The ladies and I all walk to the garden, and now it is covered in red and blue flowers. I glance at Showken and Marilyn. They both mouth "our gift to you."

There is silence, and everyone is watching us as we enter. Layern is standing on a platform in the field. It wasn't there before. The crowd separates, forming an aisle, and I walk towards Layern. The drums begin to play, and he holds out his hand for me. I want to run to him, but I keep walking. We I finally reach him he helps me up onto the platform.

"Hello, Seda."

"Hi."

"You ready?"

"Yes."

"Dance with me, and dance like it's just me and you."

The music starts a slow beat, and the people start to hum a beautiful melody. Our bodies begin a dance and Layern takes over, dipping, turning, and kissing me.

"Layern, this is beautiful. How did you get your mother to agree to change the colors?"

"It's Showken and Marilyn's celebration, and believe me,

Marilyn doesn't take any shit."

"What's going to happen?"

"I'm going to love you."

"I'm going to love you too, but what else will happen?"

"I'm going to release my fire upon you, and your hair and eyes will change to my colors."

"I'm going to lose my red hair?"

"Yes, but you will have my hair, including the texture, I'm giving you me."

We continue to dance, and my legs wrap around his waist and I start grinding. The crowd claps, enjoying our dance.

"It's time."

"Ok."

Layern's arms come around me, holding me tight, and a blue fire emanates from his entire body and begins to surround me, but something happens that I didn't expect. A red flame from my shoulders and body starts to surround him. I look into his eyes and he smiles. The heat feels so good. My hands are in his hair as my body trembles with a need for a sexual release.

"You look so beautiful, lecena."

Tears start to roll down my face. I never thought I would be free or, better yet, finding love.

"I love you, my Molla."

"Your eyes are a beautiful blue, and I think you will be happy with your hair."

We slow down our dancing and my legs slide down his body. I

feel rejuvenated, more alive than I've ever felt. All his brothers are around us. They begin to speak together... Draken, Showken, Domlen, Warton, Gemi, Hawken, Brumen, and Fewton.

'Reseda, first Young of both human and dragon, do you accept us as your brothers and protectors? We welcome you into our castle and family. You are no longer banned, but you will be honored among all, and we give you the title of Queen of female dragons. You will be known from place to place, and you shall go down in history among great kings. You are no longer alone, but you are supported by all Draglen descendants, and all the people in Cortamagen. "

When they are done speaking, I'm crying.

"It's time for us to fly. My brothers will fly a little with us, but then we are off to another place."

"Layern, I don't know how to change, I've never transformed before."

He takes my hand, and we walk off the platform and enter a field. He walks about a hundred yards away and starts to transform. His body starts to break loose, as if his bones were popping out of place, but he doesn't scream. His eyes remain on mine, and I watch as he becomes dragon in front of my eyes. His wings are dark blue and his body is the color of the ocean. He growls at me and I walk forward, coming close. I stop and he lowers his head right in front of me, our eyes meet and my beast growls, recognizing him. He covers my body with his wings, and with his sharp teeth he rips off my dress, only to find a pair of blue lace panties. His growl is more like a laugh. I can hear the brothers coming and, talking. Layern opens his mouth and breathes fire on me. It doesn't burn, but it causes my beast to react.

I fall to the ground and my body starts to bend and expand. I'm actually going to change. He blows again, and I find myself enjoying this. My arms break, and red wings come out. I allow the beast to take over and before I know it, I am standing, shorter than Layern, but as a red dragon. I try to speak, but fire comes out. It's natural. Layern growls for me to fly, taking a few steps forward. I spread my wings, and it comes naturally. I take off into the air. He is soon behind me, and the sky is filled with colorful dragons. Layern flies around me and we are playing in the air. I blow fire at some of the brothers, but soon I see Layern flying in another direction, and I follow without hesitation.

It's not long before we land in a huge field. There is water near, I can smell it. Layern transforms back into human form and I try to speak but blow fire. He moves quickly out of the way.

"Seda, please transform into human."

I lie down and concentrate and it takes some time, but eventually I work out how to transform back to human. I open my eyes to see a naked man lying next me,

"How was that, Lecena?"

"It was beautiful. Let's fly again."

"Oh, we are going to fly, but right now I just want to lose myself in you for a few days."

"Days?"

"Oh yes, I have plenty of food to keep you fueled."

"Thank you."

"No, don't thank me. You saved me from myself. I have found out what true love is, and I will never let you go."

"I'm never letting you go, either."

"Now for a real honeymoon, with no clothes."

"Mmmmm."

"You like that? Well, come on, Queen of female dragons. This prince needs you."

"I like that title."

"I love you."

"I love you more."

We kiss and make love in a field of blue flowers. I never thought I would fall in love with anyone, but I've fallen in love, gotten my freedom and become one with Prince Layern. Everything is perfect, except for my best friend, Palmer. I'll never see him again, but I can't think about anything but my Molla. Life is good.

Thank you for taking the time to read LAYERN, the third book in the Draglen Brothers series. Please enjoy the first paragraph of GEMI The next brother.

GEMI

The voice of reason is what I'm known for, but I've lost it. I'm good at keeping my brothers level headed, and giving them advice when they need it, but now, I have no one to speak with. I have stepped into forbidden territory and don't want to leave. I knew it was a bad idea, the first time I went to watch her. I don't even have the courage to speak to her, so I follow her just to see what she likes. She makes me feel out of control, and I've never kissed her. The moment I saw her, I knew she was the one, the piece I had been searching for. Who would have guessed the woman I want as my Wella would be a witch, a dragons' enemy.

I'm not going to let her go, but I will pursue her, regardless of her nature. It doesn't matter, I'm in love with her and she doesn't know it, but Shalisi is my Wella.

GEMI BK 4 The Draglen Brothers Series!

CONNECT WITH SOLEASE M BARNER

I love to connect with readers! Here is where you can find me.

https://www.facebook.com/TheDrakenBrothersASeriesBySolease
MBarner

https://www.facebook.com/solease.marksbarner

https://www.facebook.com/pages/Soleases-Sassy-Book-
Loft/584548098277710?ref_type=bookmark

If you are interested in more works by Solease M Barner, checkout
my mystery romance trilogy

"Secrets of the Ghosts-The Sleeper"

"Secrets of the Ghosts-AWAKENS"

COMING SOON!

"Secrets of the Ghosts-REDEMPTION"

ABOUT THE AUTHOR

Solease lives in a quiet area. She is a wife, and mother to a daughter. Solease loves to spend time with her family. She's been called the social butterfly by many friends. She's a huge movie buff, and loves to read books. She writes poetry on a daily basis, as a way to release stress. Solease is the author of "Secrets of the Ghosts - The Sleeper", "Secrets of the Ghosts - AWAKENS", "The Draglen Brothers Series - DRAKEN" BK 1, "The Draglen Brothers Series –SHOWKEN" BK 2 and "The Draglen Brothers Series - LAYERN" BK 3

Reviews are gold to authors! If you've enjoyed the book, would you consider rating it and reviewing it where you purchased it.

The Draglen Brothers Series

Made in the USA
Las Vegas, NV
05 April 2023

70203401R00152